The Law of

by

Jay Northcote

Copyright

Cover artist: Garrett Leigh.
Editor: Sue Adams.
The Law of Attraction © 2016 Jay Northcote.

ALL RIGHTS RESERVED

This literary work may not be reproduced or transmitted in any form or by any means, including electronic or photographic reproduction, in whole or in part, without express written permission.
This is a work of fiction and any resemblance to persons, living or dead, or business establishments, events or locales is coincidental.
The Licensed Art Material is being used for illustrative purposes only.
All Rights Are Reserved. No part of this may be used or reproduced in any manner whatsoever without written permission, except in the case of brief quotations embodied in critical articles and reviews.

Warning
This book contains material that is intended for a mature, adult audience. It contains graphic language, explicit sexual content, and adult situations.

Acknowledgements

Thank you to all the usual suspects: My pre-readers, Annabelle Jacobs and Justyna; my endlessly patient editor, Sue Adams; and my proof readers, Jen, N.R. Walker, and Posy Roberts. I couldn't do this without you.

For this book I also have a particular thank you to Joanna Chambers, who beta read this manuscript for me to check my 'legal shit' (my term, not hers). I'm immensely grateful to her for her time and expert advice.

Finally, as always, thank you to every single one of my readers for buying, reading, and otherwise supporting me.

CHAPTER ONE

Alec Rowland leaned back against the wall of the bar, a drink in his hand. He rolled his shoulders to ease the tension that had accumulated in his muscles throughout the long working day. He'd put in another twelve-hour stint at the office, and he needed to be distracted. The usual drinks with his coworkers wouldn't cut it this evening. Alec felt bad about lying to them, claiming he had a headache and pretending to go home. But it had been too long, and the pull was too strong to resist.

It was a very particular type of distraction he was looking for tonight.

Alec picked out the guy as he watched from his place in the shadows. He was average height and slimly built; his hair was an indeterminate colour in the dim lights at the edge of the still mostly empty dance floor—light brown, perhaps, or maybe blond? It was his smile that drew Alec's attention. He was with a group of friends, who looked like they could be students—young, casual, carefree. They were talking and laughing, and when this guy grinned at something a girl said, his face lit up.

Alec watched them for a while, sipping at his whisky while he assessed his chances. As they were in a gay bar, it was likely that the object of his interest swung his way, but he didn't look like he was here to hook up. He didn't have the roving eye that Alec knew meant an easy target. He was focused on his friends, not eyeing up the talent.

Alec liked a challenge.

His opportunity came when the guy broke away from the group and headed to the bar. His arse was as beautiful as his smile, curving sweetly at the top of his slender legs. Alec followed him, draining the last of his whisky as he went. He stepped in behind his quarry, noting he was taller than the younger man by a good couple of inches. Alec's gaze skated over the snug T-shirt that showed a lean frame and wide shoulders tapering to slim hips. A flash of skin above the waistband of his jeans made Alec long to touch, to run a fingertip along that smooth expanse and make him shiver.

Alec raised his eyes and found blue ones looking back at him from the mirror behind the bar. A smirk curved the guy's full, pink lips as he met Alec's eyes, then he turned slowly around to lean back against the bar. He folded his arms over his flat belly and looked Alec up and down appraisingly.

"Are you going to offer to buy me a drink, then?" He raised his eyebrows. "Or didn't I pass muster?"

Cheeky. Alec could handle cheeky.

"What are you having?"

"Rum and Coke, please." His face remained expressionless.

Alec caught the eye of one of the guys behind the bar and leaned in to make himself heard over the background noise. "Double rum and Coke, and double scotch—neat, no ice." He could smell the other man's sweat, fresh and clean. Alec's cock started to react. He put his hand in his pocket and made a subtle adjustment as he drew back. He was still in his suit, and the fabric didn't do much to hide a hard-on. Good thing he was wearing snug boxer briefs to keep it in check.

His companion was still watching him, seemingly waiting for him to make his move. Alec felt irrationally irritated. This wasn't how it was supposed to go. Even though he only did it occasionally, picking up men was easy for Alec. Buying a drink was more than he usually bothered to do for the twinks he hooked up with when he was in the mood for a warm body to fuck. Alec was well aware of his own attractiveness and used it to his advantage. A crook of a finger, a tilt of his head, or even just a look was usually enough to make them come running.

But this guy didn't seem to know the rules of the game.

"Strong, silent type, huh?" He suddenly grinned at Alec, all neat white teeth and dimples. "You could start by telling me your name. Mine's Ed."

"Alec." He handed a note to the barman as he came back with their drinks. "Keep the change."

"Cheers, mate." The barman winked as he pocketed the tip.

Ed's eyebrows lifted. "Change from a twenty? You must have money to burn."

"Something like that." Alec let his gaze rake deliberately down Ed, examining him from the front this time. His arms were still folded over his chest and his T-shirt had ridden up enough to expose a feathered line of hair on his belly, leading down to a nice-looking package in obscenely tight skinny jeans. "I hope you bottom?"

Ed blinked and choked on his mouthful of rum and Coke. Alec suppressed the urge to grin, enjoying the fact that Ed had momentarily lost his cool.

"I've been known to," Ed replied, rallying. He licked his lips.

"Good." Alec held his gaze, noting with satisfaction that Ed's pupils had blown wide and his lips parted as Alec looked at them. God, he had a pretty mouth. Alec lifted his glass and downed his drink. The burn of the whisky tore through him and made his nerves tingle with anticipation. He needed a good fuck; it had been too long. "Drink up, then."

"You're an arrogant bastard, aren't you?" Ed frowned, looking at Alec as though he were a puzzle to be solved.

"But you want me anyway." Alec stepped close, right into Ed's space. He reached out and cupped the bulge in Ed's jeans, tracing the shape of his cock through the material with his fingertips.

Ed sucked in a breath and his hips arched into the touch. He hesitated, a small frown marring his brow. Then he seemed to reach a decision. "Fuck... okay. But I need to go and tell my friends I'm leaving so they won't worry about me."

"Okay." Alec squeezed his dick again before releasing it. "I'll wait by the exit. Don't be long."

They sat in the taxi in awkward silence. Alec wasn't one for public displays, but with Ed wriggling in his seat and adjusting his erection approximately every minute, his self-control was sorely tried.

"I know it's a cliché," Ed said, "but I don't normally do this." He didn't turn to look at Alec as he spoke. He watched the traffic out of the taxi window as they sped through the dark London streets.

It was past eleven on a Friday night, and people were spilling out of pubs and heading into clubs, ready to party into Saturday morning and start the weekend with a bang. Alec was planning on starting his with a whole different type of bang. He imagined Ed spread out for him, that gorgeous arse open and ready. The damn taxi couldn't move fast enough.

"I don't care what you normally do." Alec put his hand on Ed's thigh, feeling the tension of fight or flight simmering there. He stroked, trying to make him relax. He didn't want Ed to change his mind.

"I take it this isn't your first time to pick up a random in a club, then?" Ed turned to look at him.

Alec held his gaze for a moment but didn't reply. He wasn't about to justify his lifestyle to a stranger. He leaned forward, speaking loudly to the driver through the glass. "It's the next left."

The driver waved his hand to acknowledge that he'd heard.

"They have to take a test." Ed said, amused. "I'm sure he knows where he's going."

"It cuts off a corner," Alec snapped back. "And they usually miss it. I should know."

"Impatient, are we?" Ed teased.

Alec ignored him. He'd wipe that sly smile away soon enough; it was hard to grin knowingly with your lips stretched round a dick.

"I should have known you'd live somewhere posh," Ed commented as they climbed the steps to Alec's building. The facade was beautiful: classic Georgian architecture. It had originally been one house but was now converted into three flats. "The rent on this must be astronomical." He held his thin jacket tightly around him, shivering in the freezing January air. His breath made vapour clouds as he spoke.

"I own it."

"Of course you do."

Alec unlocked the front door and led Ed inside. Ed pushed the door shut behind him, but Alec paused to check he'd closed it properly.

"I do know how to close a door."

Alec could practically hear the eye-roll. "Good." He crossed the hallway to the door to his flat and unlocked it. "Do you know how to suck cock as well?"

Ed stepped up behind him, his feet echoing on the tiled floor, and when he replied, his voice was close enough to raise the hairs on the back of Alec's neck. "Oh yeah, I think you'll find I'm rather good at that."

Ed got his hands on Alec as soon as they'd passed through the door of his flat. Ed reached under Alec's suit jacket, untucking his shirt and going for his fly while Alec was still closing the door and turning on the light switch.

"Fuck," Alec gasped as Ed got his hand inside his underwear and gripped his erection. He hadn't been expecting Ed to make the first move, but maybe he should have been. Ed had managed to surprise him at nearly every turn already, so why would this be any different?

"You're all sticky already." Ed's breath was hot on his neck. "That's so hot."

Alec turned and looked into Ed's face. Ed's blue eyes were dark and hungry, and his lips pink and wet as though he'd been biting them. Alec almost leaned in to kiss him, but he held himself back, trying to stay in control of the situation. He put his hands on Ed's shoulders and pushed him down.

"Get down there and taste it, then." His voice was rough, unfamiliar in his throat. Something about Ed was really getting to him. He had rarely wanted anyone as intensely as he wanted Ed. He needed that mouth on him. He needed to come.

Ed went willingly as Alec fumbled with his trousers and underwear, pushing them down below his balls. When his cock sprang free, Ed was waiting. He looked up at Alec with a wicked gleam in his eyes and slid his slightly parted lips over the head, smearing precome like lip gloss and making Alec grit his teeth with the effort not to moan.

Alec reached down and rubbed the pad of his thumb over Ed's bottom lip, then pressed down, opening his mouth for his cock. "Take it," he growled. "Fucking tease."

He grabbed Ed's hair firmly with his other hand and held him still as he pushed his cock into the wet heat of Ed's mouth. Ed opened up, his gaze still on Alec's as his tongue lapped at the underside of Alec's cock. He closed his lips around the sensitive head and sucked as Alec pushed in deep, seeing how much Ed could take. It turned out he could take it all, and Alec wasn't small. He nudged the back of Ed's throat and felt the constriction as

Ed gagged slightly before adjusting to the intrusion.

"That's it. That's good." Alec leaned back against the door and watched as Ed took over and started to move, taking Alec deep in long, slow pulls. Ed's eyes fluttered shut, and he looked lost in it, blissed out by the feel of a cock in his mouth.

Alec closed his eyes too; the sight of Ed was almost too much for him to handle. He groaned in protest when Ed pulled off, but Ed's hand gripped his cock and his mouth was on Alec's balls instead, soothing them with ticklish licks and kisses.

"You taste good," Ed muttered, mouthing at Alec's balls and nuzzling into the crease of his groin. "And you smell amazing. So fucking sexy."

Alec moved his hips mindlessly, fucking his cock into Ed's fist. He was close now. It had been weeks since he'd done this—months even. If he came now, he'd be able to enjoy fucking Ed later without worrying about it being over too soon.

Ed licked back up Alec's shaft and sucked him in again. He held the base of Alec's cock in his fist while his tongue worked its magic. He licked around the crown and dipped it under the foreskin with each upward stroke of his hand.

The sound of a zip distracted Alec. He looked down to see Ed with his own dick in his hand, stroking it in time with the movement of his mouth on Alec.

Alec was so close now; he could barely force the words out. "Don't come yet. Wait."

He wanted to be the one to make Ed come.

Ed moaned, but his hand stopped moving, gripping his cock tightly. The thrill of him obeying the order brought Alec right to the edge. Ed looked up at Alec and their gazes locked.

"Good," Alec gritted out as he felt himself start to come, balls drawing up, muscles tensing. "Oh fuck. *Yes*."

Ed pulled off right at the last minute and used his hand to work Alec's cock, teasing out every drop as Alec emptied his balls over Ed's face and throat. The sight of his come striping that pretty face made Alec come harder and longer than he had in ages, muscles jerking and twitching until his legs nearly gave out.

When Ed finally released his cock, Alec swiped at the white streaks on Ed's cheek with his thumb. "You're a fucking mess."

Ed used his fingertips to clear come from his eyelashes before opening his eyes and grinning up at Alec. "I'm a hot mess, though."

Alec snorted in amusement. Then he asked, "Was that a safe-sex thing? Or are facials a kink for you?"

Ed got to his feet. "A bit of both."

"I was tested a couple of months ago. All negative. Just so you know." Alec tucked his cock back into his boxers, but he left the fly of his trousers open. They'd be coming off soon enough.

"But you pick up boys in clubs on a regular basis."

"Not that regularly, actually." Alec pulled his handkerchief out of the pocket of his suit jacket and handed it to Ed for his face. "Anyway—how about you? If I suck you off, can I swallow?" Alec's gaze dropped to Ed's erection where it bobbed, sticking proudly out of his fly. It jumped at Alec's words. Alec didn't usually reciprocate; he normally just fucked the guys he picked up, but he wanted Ed in his mouth, wanted to feel him come on his tongue.

"Yes." Ed's voice was husky and raw with desire, or maybe from Alec's cock in his throat.

Alec weighed the risks. His instinct was to trust Ed, and his instincts were usually good. His libido won the battle. "Bedroom, then. I want you naked." Alec gestured down the corridor. "This way."

Ed whistled when Alec switched on the lamp beside the bed. "This place is amazing. But where the heck is all your stuff?"

Alec shrugged as he let his gaze skim over the stripped pine floorboards, the clear surfaces of his chest of drawers, the double doors of a built-in wardrobe. "I hate clutter, especially in here. I have an office for my work, and my living room has all my books and DVDs in it. This room is for dressing and sleeping."

"And fucking?" Ed met his gaze and reached for the hem of his T-shirt. He stripped it off in one swift movement. His body was pale gold in the muted light; slender, yet taut and toned. The just-visible ripples of his flat stomach muscles led down to the vee of his hips where his jeans hung open. His cock jutted out of a trimmed nest of golden brown curls.

"That too, sometimes." A smile crept over Alec's face despite himself, and Ed grinned back at him, open and easy.

Alec slid his suit jacket off and crossed the room. He tossed it over the armchair that stood in the bay window, and then drew the dark brown velvet curtains across. He heard the rustle of clothing behind him, and when he turned back, Ed was naked.

Alec approached, working his tie loose with his fingers before starting on the buttons of his shirt. Ed stared at him, his gaze flickering from Alec's eyes to his lips and back.

"You looked damn good in that suit—" Ed reached for the tie and used the ends to pull Alec close. "—but you look even hotter like this, all dishevelled and horny."

Ed stared at Alec's lips and swallowed, licking his own as he did so, then stepped closer and tilted his face up, increasing the steady pressure on Alec's tie. Alec allowed himself to be pulled down into the kiss, parting his lips and letting Ed lick into his mouth and suck on his tongue. Ed kissed like he sucked cock, with enthusiasm and considerable expertise. Alec could taste his come on Ed's lips. A slow burn of arousal started to build in his balls again.

He'd chosen well tonight.

Alec kissed back, exploring the sleek interior of Ed's mouth as he brought his hands up to cup Ed's face and take some control back. Ed's skin was soft, with just a faint hint of stubble along his jaw that rubbed against Alec's as they lost themselves in the slide and suck of mouth on mouth.

Ed had his hands on Alec's shirt buttons now, unfastening those that were still done up so that he could push the shirt off Alec's shoulders. Ed pressed close and groaned as the dark hair on Alec's chest scratched over his nipples. He ground his cock into Alec's hip.

"God," Ed breathed as he broke the kiss. "Fuck... *please*. I need to come."

"Get on the bed." Alec toed off his shoes and stepped out of his trousers, taking his socks and underwear with them. He tossed the whole lot aside. He knew Ed would be watching. When he turned, Ed had pushed the duvet down and was lying on the sheets with his hand wrapped around his cock, stroking himself slowly. His gaze raked over Alec's body appreciatively.

"Jesus, you're hot." Ed's hand kept moving as he spoke. "You're completely and utterly my type: tall, dark, and brooding—and ridiculously sexy. I'll be really pissed off if I wake up and find this is all a wet dream."

Alec grinned. "I'm pretty sure I'm real." He paused to fish a condom and some lube out of the bedside drawer, and then climbed onto the bed and pushed Ed's knees apart so that he could lie between them. Alec ran his hands up Ed's thighs. Blond hairs tickled his palms, and Ed shivered under his touch. "Get your hand off your cock," Alec ordered.

"Sadist." But Ed moved his hand, gripping the sheets as he waited.

His cock was flushed dark pink at the tip and leaving a sticky trail on the skin of his belly. It was gorgeous, slender and gently curving, and so hard that Ed must be aching. His balls were high and tight, pulled in close to his body, and almost hairless. Alec's gaze followed the dark seam back along his taint and into the cleft behind.

Alec's cock was hard again, thick and heavy between his thighs. He'd be ready to fuck soon, but he decided Ed deserved to come first.

He lowered himself down onto the pristine white sheets. The cotton brushed deliciously against his growing erection as he shuffled back into position. Ed spread his thighs wider, eager for Alec's touch.

He started by licking that tantalising seam, his tongue flat against the sensitive skin behind Ed's balls. Ed's cock jerked as he hissed in a breath, and Alec smiled. He repeated the motion and breathed in the musky scent of Ed's balls. Alec's mouth watered, and he moved a little higher, licking and sucking on the soft skin and wrinkled sac. Ed writhed and moaned, his hips arching up as though he couldn't control the movement, but Alec kept his hands firm on his thighs, holding him down.

When he finally licked a wet stripe up Ed's cock, it flexed under his tongue and another drop of clear fluid pulsed out. Alec used his hand at the base and lifted it so that he could close his lips around the head and suck Ed clean. The sweet, salty taste made Alec's cock throb and he swirled his tongue around, making Ed whimper and buck against the weight of Alec's hand on his hip.

"Alec!" It was the first time he'd used Alec's name.

Alec moved a hand up, reaching for Ed's parted lips. He pressed two fingers against the plushness of his lower lip, and Ed sucked them in greedily, using his tongue to make them wet.

Alec took Ed's cock deep, sucking him into the back of his throat as he pulled his fingers out of Ed's mouth. He reached down to circle Ed's hole, his spit-wet fingers sliding easily over the puckered skin. He felt the muscle give as Ed opened up for him, and one finger slipped into the tight, grasping heat. Alec hummed around Ed's cock, drawing his mouth up the shaft and popping his lips repeatedly over the rim. His lips were wet and messy with spit and the precome Ed was leaking. Ed's breath was coming in ragged gasps, and he moaned and swore as Alec thrust into him with two fingers now, curling and reaching to rub on his prostate. "Fuck, Alec, fuck… *yes*."

Ed's arse clenched tight around Alec's fingers, pulsing to the beat of his orgasm as his cock spurted and filled Alec's mouth. Alec kept sucking and fucking Ed with his fingers until Ed put his hands on Alec's head and pulled him away. "Stop now. It's too much."

Alec swallowed, licking his lips and watching Ed as he eased his fingers out of him. Ed's body was lax and floppy with release, his face flushed and glowing. He already looked fucked out, and Alec hadn't finished with him yet.

Alec sat back on his knees and gripped his cock. He was hard and ready to go and he hoped Ed would be up for more. "Are you going to take my cock now?" Alec stroked himself, feeling the heat pooling in his groin at the touch of his hand. He couldn't wait to get inside that tight arse.

"That's what I'm here for," Ed replied with a tilt of his eyebrow. "Show me what you've got."

Alec reached for a condom and rolled it over his cock. Ed watched his hand, his expression hungry.

"Turn over." Alec had no desire for eye contact and kissing during the act. He wanted to dominate, to control, to lose himself in Ed's hot body without distraction.

Ed's face was very distracting.

Ed flipped over, rising up on his hands and knees. God, his arse was gorgeous: smooth and firm and beautifully rounded. Alec admired it as he slicked his fingers and brought them down to stretch Ed out a little more. "Are you ready?" He lined up the head of his cock and waited.

"Yeah." Ed looked over his shoulder, meeting Alec's gaze.

Alec found himself unable to look away as he started to inch his way in. Ed was tight and the pressure was intense, but Ed relaxed and pushed back onto Alec's cock, groaning and finally dropping his head as Alec gave it all to him. He held tight to Ed's hips as he paused. Ed was panting, his ribcage expanding with every ragged breath. Alec leaned forward, pressing his lips to the bumps of Ed's spine, to his shoulder blades. He nipped at the flesh of Ed's shoulder and then licked, tasting the musky sweet-salt of Ed's skin on his tongue. "Okay?" he murmured, then bit down again.

"Yeah. Get on with it." The teasing tone was belied by the hoarse quality of Ed's voice, the needy edge giving him away.

The challenge prickled under Alec's skin and made him pull back more swiftly than he'd intended, slamming back in so his balls swung against Ed's and their skin slapped together.

"Fuck!" The word was knocked out of Ed and he nearly lost his balance, slipping down onto his elbows rather than his hands.

Alec's fingers curled into his hips, keeping them up as he carried on, fucking into Ed's beautiful arse with long, deep strokes. "Okay?" he asked again.

Ed's voice was less steady this time, his words disjointed by the force of Alec's thrusts. "Fine. Just fuck me. Assume I'm fine… unless I say otherwise."

So that's how it's going to be.

Alec gritted his teeth and went for it. He wanted to break through the protective shell of cheek and attitude that encased Ed like armour. He put one hand on Ed's shoulder for leverage and curled the other hand around the crest of Ed's hipbone. Each stroke sounded like a blow as their bodies collided, skin on skin. Ed grunted, pushing back to meet him. Alec could feel the squeeze of the muscles around his cock as Ed gripped him, his body clinging to Alec's dick and trying to hold him there each time he plunged in, balls-deep.

"Fuck. That's good." Ed sounded wrecked.

Suddenly Alec wished he could see his face after all. He pulled out with no warning and slapped Ed's arse with a loud *crack*. "Turn over."

"God, are you always this bossy?" Ed bitched. He moved anyway, flipping over onto his back again, and then he pulled his knees up towards his chest, offering himself up. He moaned as Alec slammed back in and started to fuck him again.

Alec was close now, but he wanted to make Ed come again first. He reached for Ed's cock and gripped it, stroking smoothly, thumbing at the head.

Ed was slippery in his hand, and he whimpered at Alec's touch. "Faster," Ed gritted out. "I'm nearly there."

Alec wasn't the only bossy one in this bed, but he didn't have enough breath to point it out right now. He wasn't sure if Ed meant him to be faster with his hand or with his dick in Ed's arse, so he sped up the pace of both. Sweat trickled down his back as he jerked his hips harder, faster; tension built in his balls and spread fast. His hand flew over Ed's cock, sticky and slick.

"Fuck. Yes, Jesus, fuck, fuck, *fuck*...." A stream of curses spilled from Ed's bitten-red lips as his body went taut and his hips bucked. White drops splattered on his chest and belly as he convulsed, almost forcing Alec's cock out with the uncontrollable arch of his spine. But Alec released Ed's still-spurting dick and used both hands to hold Ed's legs on his shoulders, and he pushed in deep. The clench of Ed's internal muscles, like a fist around him, pulled Alec over the edge, milking his release as he stilled and shuddered. His eyes fluttered shut, and the scent of their sex invaded his senses as he moaned, still coming, chasing the last perfect jolt of pleasure as it rippled through him.

When he opened his eyes, Ed was looking up at him and grinning, still breathless.

Alec let Ed pull him down and crush their mouths together in a greedy kiss that gradually turned into something softer until Alec broke away, avoiding Ed's gaze.

"I'll get you something to clean up with." He pulled out, removed the condom, and knotted it as he padded across the floorboards to the door.

He took a little longer in the bathroom than he needed, used the toilet, and brushed his teeth before running some warm water on a flannel for Ed. Alec felt the bone-deep weariness of another long week soak through him now the high of his climax had passed. He just wanted to get rid of Ed so that he could sleep alone as usual. He'd shower the scent of Ed off his skin in the morning.

Alec looked at himself in the mirror as he squeezed out the cloth. His hair was still rumpled by Ed's hands, and his lips were tender and flushed from their last kiss. Yet, when he gazed into the dark eyes of his reflection, he saw loneliness staring back.

When he returned to the bedroom, he found Ed exactly where he'd left him — sprawled on the rumpled sheets with come drying on his belly. Only now he was fast asleep.

"You have to be joking," Alec muttered. He raised his voice. "Ed, wake up!" No response. "Oh, for fuck's sake."

Alec sighed and knelt over Ed's sleeping form. He wiped Ed's belly perfunctorily, avoiding his dick, which lay soft and innocent on his thigh. Ed stirred and mumbled something unintelligible as Alec slid the cloth over his skin, and then Ed rolled onto his side, pulling a pillow down and snuggling into it.

Alec's lips twitched in amusement tinged with exasperation. *Fuck it.* One night of bed sharing wouldn't kill him. As long as Ed wasn't expecting cuddling or breakfast in the morning, they'd be good.

Alec climbed into the bed beside Ed, turned the lamp off, and pulled the duvet over them. He lay on his back in the darkness, watching the familiar, shadowy contours of his bedroom emerge from the blackness as his eyes adjusted. No part of his body was in contact with Ed's, but he could feel the warmth of him nonetheless.

Ed sighed and shifted beside him, his breathing slow and steady.

Alec's eyes fluttered shut despite the tension in his body. Slowly, imperceptibly, he relaxed. His body became heavy and his breath fell into a rhythm that matched Ed's as sleep pulled him under.

CHAPTER TWO

Ed drifted slowly into consciousness through the thick, deep fog of contented sleep that enveloped him.

The first thing he was aware of was heat that made his skin prickle with sweat. He shifted, trying to push the covers down, but then realised he had a hot body pressed up against him and a heavy arm wrapped around his torso. The body behind him made a snuffling sound and the arm around him squeezed, pulling him back more tightly against bare skin. Ed froze, blinking in the darkness as his sleep-scrambled brain woke slowly, piecing together the events of the evening.

There had been drinking with friends and loud music. Ed cast his mind back, searching for details to explain his current situation. A gay bar... a ridiculously sexy-looking man with dark hair buying him a drink... Ed flirting back....

Fuck.

He was still in bed with the guy from the bar. *Alec.* The seriously hot, totally out of his league guy from the club. His dick tingled and swelled as he remembered Alec's cock in his throat, Alec's hands and mouth on him, Alec fucking him into the mattress he was now lying on. The memories came pouring into his consciousness in great and vivid detail. The muscles in his arse clenched reflexively and the well-fucked sensitivity made Ed grin.

But why was he still here? Alec hadn't seemed like the cuddly type. Right from the start, Ed had assumed this was going to be a one-time thing. His instincts told him that, and Alec had done nothing to make him believe otherwise. Ed thought Alec was the type of guy who would have chucked him out as soon as they were done fucking.

He thought back. He remembered Alec pulling out of him and going to the bathroom… and then nothing.

Oops.

Ed was prone to falling asleep after coming, especially after a spectacular fuck like that. He could only assume he'd crashed out and Alec had taken pity on him—or been unable to wake him. It was pitch black in the room, so was presumably still the middle of the night.

Oh, well. Alec appeared to be okay with him being here.

Ed shifted experimentally again, still too hot in Alec's arms. As he wriggled, his arse pushed back against an unmistakable hardness, and Alec hummed in his sleep, moving his hips against Ed's arse. Unable to resist temptation, Ed pressed back instinctively, his cock thickening and hardening at the contact. He moved his hips gently in a subtle rhythm that made Alec rub against him, his warm breath coming faster against the nape of Ed's neck as his cock slid against the crack of Ed's arse and the small of his back. Ed moved his hand down, reaching for his own erection. He gripped it, pressing forward into his fist, and then back against Alec's hot cock in a lazy, rocking motion.

Alec moaned, a rough sound in his throat, and the arm clamped around Ed's chest moved. Alec ran his hand over Ed's belly and down to Ed's hand, wrapped around his prick. "Ed?" Alec sounded confused, uncertain.

"Right name, well done," Ed replied, still jerking himself off slowly.

Alec's cock was leaking, leaving sticky wetness in the small of Ed's back.

"Let me." Alec pried Ed's fingers away and replaced them with his own. "Fuck, you're so hard." His breath washed over Ed's neck again, and he followed the words with gentle kisses as he rocked his hips faster. "You feel good." Alec's voice was drunk with sleep, but his body was definitely with the programme. "I want to fuck you again… but I don't want to stop this."

Ed shivered and moaned. He didn't want Alec to stop either. He imagined how it would feel if Alec could just press right into him now, filling him up and fucking him senseless again. He mentally cursed the need for condoms and lube.

"Try it like this." Ed drew his knees up a little, lifting his upper leg slightly to allow Alec access. He reached around and repositioned Alec's cock so that he was thrusting into the channel between Ed's thighs, and then he clamped them closed again. It was sweaty there and still slippery with lube from earlier.

"Fuck," Alec muttered, thrusting and fucking into the tight space Ed had made for him.

His cock dragged back over Ed's perineum and forward to nudge his balls with every stroke as Alec's hand on his cock squeezed with perfect pressure.

Nothing about it was rushed this time. Earlier everything had been fast and furious between them, a battle of wills as they fought each other for control. This time it was lazy and leisurely, a steady build of heat and want that curled in Ed's belly and pooled in his balls, syrupy-slow and delicious. Alec sucked searing kisses on Ed's neck and shoulders, his body warm and close, surrounding him as Alec forced his cock into the hot, damp crevice between Ed's thighs. Ed relished the sounds Alec was making: broken, desperate sounds, almost like sobs. He wished he could see his face. He'd like to see Alec like this, his tight control abandoned, swept away by the force of his desire.

Alec groaned, a pained sound, and bit down on the skin of Ed's neck hard, his hips jerking. The hot rush of wetness between Ed's thighs and the feeling of Alec shuddering behind him were what made Ed come, more than Alec's hand on his cock. He cried out, pleasure flooding him as his cock pulsed and spilled in Alec's grip. Alec stroked him through it, his lips and tongue soothing the bite on Ed's neck in unspoken apology, gentle now.

Alec released Ed's cock when it softened, but he didn't roll away immediately. His arm was still heavy over Ed's flank as he spoke. "If I go and get another flannel, will you be asleep again when I get back?"

Ed chuckled. "Quite possibly. But I can go. I need a piss anyway, and my mouth feels like something died in it."

"That's what you get for crashing out in other people's beds without brushing your teeth first." Alec sounded amused rather than irritated. "The bathroom's the next door along the corridor. Flannels are in the cupboard under the sink. You can go first. You're stickier than me."

It was a challenge negotiating a strange flat in almost total darkness, but Ed managed to find the bathroom without tripping over or crashing into anything. The sudden glare off the white tiles and sink as he switched on the bathroom light made him wince and squint until his eyes adjusted.

He emptied his bladder as a matter of urgency and then cleaned off as much of the come as he could manage. That had been a fun little interlude, but thigh-fucking was a messy business. Thankfully his balls and crack were well trimmed, otherwise there was no way he would manage to get the spunk off without a shower, and somehow he didn't think Alec would want him to make himself too much at home.

Finally he did the best he could to freshen his mouth up a bit with a finger and some toothpaste. He rinsed and spat and then studied his reflection. Leaning closer, he tilted his head to the side. "Bugger," he muttered.

Alec had left a dark red mark sucked into the pale skin of Ed's neck. It was in the exact spot where it would show above his collar when he started his new job on Monday. What a way to make a good first impression in the workplace.

Ed shook his head as he turned off the light and stepped back out into the darkness of the hallway. He paused for a moment, letting his eyes adjust, and went back into Alec's room. "What time is it anyway?" he asked as Alec got out of bed.

"Just after three."

"Ugh."

"Go back to sleep." Alec closed the bedroom door behind him.

This time Ed was still awake when Alec climbed back into the bed beside him. Ed was lying on his back. Alec settled on his side, facing away; he didn't say anything.

Ed wondered what Alec would do if Ed tried to snuggle up, and his lips twitched as he imagined the possible reactions. Yeah. He wasn't going to risk it. "Good night," he whispered instead.

"Night," Alec replied softly.

When Ed woke in the morning, he had the bed to himself. There was a warm patch next to him, so Alec couldn't have been gone long. The rushing of water pipes suggested Alec was showering. Ed sighed. It didn't look like a leisurely Saturday-morning shag was on the cards, then. Shame. After their little interlude in the small hours, Ed had hoped Alec might not be in too much of a hurry to get rid of him the next day.

A clock on the bedside table showed it was just after eight. Ed yawned and stretched, scratching his belly. It still felt distinctly crusty despite his middle-of-the-night ablutions.

Ed got out of bed and padded over to the window. The floorboards were chilly on his bare feet. He peeked through the heavy velvet curtains and saw a well-tended garden at the back of the building and more large houses behind that were similar to this one. He opened the curtains a little to let some light in, but not wide enough to give Alec's neighbours a show. The sun was out, but frost dusted the lawn outside. Ed's breath fogged the glass.

The sound of the water stopped abruptly with the clanking of old-fashioned plumbing. Not wanting to be caught standing naked at the window, Ed hastily retrieved his clothes from the floor where he'd shucked them off the night before. He was just fastening his jeans when the bedroom door opened and Alec came in, wearing nothing but a pair of skintight charcoal boxer briefs.

Jesus Christ. He was even more gorgeous in daylight.

Tall, dark, and handsome was a start but didn't even begin to cover it. Alec was broad and lean with the perfect amount of muscle on his frame. He didn't have the ripped look of someone who spent hours watching himself in the mirror in the gym, but his body was beautiful and spoke subtly of grace and power.

Best of all was his body hair. Ed was a big fan of a hairy chest and constantly bemoaned the fact they were so unfashionable these days. All those should-be-hairy Hollywood stars and underwear models who waxed and shaved made Ed want to cry. He'd give anything to have more than the few paltry hairs that grew around each nipple on his own smooth chest. He did shave those off because in isolation they looked ridiculous.

Alec's chest was glorious. Dark hair scattered evenly over his powerful pectorals, then narrowed into a trail of softer-looking hair on his belly that twisted and twined into a dark arrow leading down to his groin—like Ed needed a sign. *Damn.* He wished he'd taken more time to explore Alec's stunning body last night. He would have liked to have licked and nuzzled that chest for a while before cutting to the main event. What a wasted opportunity. Maybe he should ask Alec for his number….

Alec cleared his throat. Ed's cheeks and ears flamed hot as he realised he was ogling shamelessly. He snapped his eyes up and met Alec's gaze. Alec's hazel eyes were compelling in daylight, but his expression was flat and unamused. Ed blushed harder.

Alec turned his back on Ed and went to the built-in wardrobe to pick out some clothes. Ed noticed faint lines of pale scars that marred Alec's back in the light from the window. They striped his shoulder blades, cutting across the smooth skin. Ed frowned as he wondered what could have caused them.

"I'm afraid I have to be somewhere this morning." Alec stepped into some expensive-looking chinos, pulling them up over his muscular legs. "I'm sorry to turf you out."

He didn't sound sorry at all. He sounded cold, distant, and uncomfortable.

A sick feeling of disappointment settled in Ed's belly like a stone. Not that he had really expected anything different when he came home with Alec last night, but still. In the darkness he thought he'd felt a connection, a momentary tenderness that made him hopeful. Now, in the cold light of day, he felt foolish and cursed his overactive imagination.

Ed gritted his teeth and took a deep breath before replying. "No worries. I need to head to the gym anyway, and I have lunch plans."

Nobody liked to feel utterly disposable, and the offer of a cup of tea or coffee would have softened the rejection a little. This was exactly why Ed didn't do one-night stands anymore, because on the odd occasion he had in the past, he always felt crap about it in the aftermath. No matter how good the sex was, it wasn't worth feeling like shit the next morning. Even when you parted on good terms, there was something uncomfortable about the whole morning-after disconnect after spending a night with someone.

Ed pulled his T-shirt over his head and sat awkwardly on the edge of the bed to pull on his socks and shoes. The sheets were rumpled and smelled of sex. The memory of Alec thrusting between his thighs assaulted him, their bodies wrapped close as Alec kissed his neck and shoulders, over and over. The intimacy of that moment seemed a million miles away now, and Ed fleetingly wondered if he'd dreamed it. He pushed the images away and stood. "I'll let myself out."

Alec was still buttoning his shirt. "Okay, sure." He looked up and met Ed's gaze.

There was a flash of something in his dark eyes. Regret—or discomfort? Ed didn't give a fuck right then. He just wanted to get out of there and get home so he could wash Alec off his skin.

"Goodbye, then." Ed suppressed the ridiculous British instinct to say thank you. *Thank for sucking my cock, thank you for fucking me, thank you for three amazing orgasms… but fuck you for making me feel like nothing in the morning.*

Alec's lips curved in a poor attempt at a smile. "Bye." His eyes gave nothing away.

That was it, then. Goodbye. Not even a half-hearted "See you around." Ed had been given the brush-off plenty of times before. He didn't know why he was letting Alec get to him any more than usual. Somehow Alec had fooled him into thinking there was something special there during those stolen moments of intimacy in the darkness, but maybe it had all been in Ed's head? There was certainly nothing to show for it this morning.

Ed turned on his heel and walked away. As he let himself out of Alec's flat, he resisted the childish urge to slam the door behind him—but only just.

Ed called Fiona as soon as he got on the Tube.

"I'm on my way home. Can we go out for breakfast? I'm starving and I need to be spoiled."

"Oh dear," she said sympathetically. "Morning-after blues?"

"Something like that, yeah."

"Okay. I'll see you back here soon, and then we can go out and you can tell me all about him."

Fiona sat curled up on the sofa with a mug in her hands when Ed let himself into the flat they shared. They'd been flatmates during their time at university, but then Ed had moved to Manchester for two years to complete his training with a firm there. When he came back to London last month after spending a few months travelling abroad, he'd needed somewhere to live while he took some temp jobs and applied for something permanent in the area he wanted to work in. He'd slept on Fiona's sofa for while, but then her other flatmate got a job in Birmingham, so Ed had moved back in officially.

She studied him over the rim of her mug. "You look like something the cat dragged in."

"Good morning to you too. Is that coffee?"

She rolled her eyes and offered it to him. "Have it. I'll make myself some more."

"Thanks. You're an angel, Fi." Ed came and took the mug. He sat beside her and gulped it down in a few grateful swallows. It was delicious: the real thing, not crappy instant stuff, the perfect temperature, and exactly what he needed.

"I know." Fiona leaned in and kissed his cheek. "I'm going to get dressed. You go and shower and make yourself look less debauched. It's currently obvious from a hundred paces that you've been out all night and thoroughly fucked. And don't even get me started on the mark on your neck. It looks as though you've been mauled."

Ed chuckled, but the sound of wry amusement stuck in his throat. "Nice of him to give me something to remember him by, eh?"

"Well, at least you can't be pregnant."

Ed laughed. "That's true."

Once they'd found somewhere to sit and the waitress had taken their orders, Fiona folded her arms on the table and fixed Ed with her penetrating blue gaze.

"So, spill. Why are you looking like someone pissed in your cornflakes when you should be glowing in a post-sex high? I saw him. He looked gorgeous. Was he crap in bed?"

"No!"

"Were *you* crap in bed?"

"Fuck you, no!" Ed retorted indignantly. He recalled the ecstatic expression on Alec's face when he came. "He didn't have any complaints. I don't know, I...." He flushed, lowering his voice and feeling foolish. "I guess I thought there was a connection, more than just a fuck, and I hoped maybe he'd ask for my number or something. But it must have just been me, because he could hardly look at me in the morning. It was horrible."

Ed looked down, fiddling with the cutlery on the table. He picked up a spoon and studied his inverted reflection, not wanting to see the sympathy in Fiona's eyes. "It's stupid, really. I knew it was only going to be a one-night stand."

"It's not stupid." Fiona reached across and took his free hand, giving it a squeeze. She threaded her fingers into his, and he looked up again. "It always sucks when you want more and you can't have it."

"Yeah, well. He's obviously a cold-hearted git anyway, so I'm better off without him. But why don't I ever meet any nice guys?"

Fiona raised her eyebrows. "Simon? Matt? Ring any bells?"

"Okay, okay. Why don't I ever meet any nice guys who hold my interest for more than a couple of months?"

"I don't know, sweetie. Maybe you haven't met the right one yet."

The waitress interrupted them with their breakfasts and coffees, and Ed let the subject drop. He wanted to push Alec out of his mind. He was never going to see him again anyway.

"So," Fiona asked as she loaded her fork with bacon and scrambled egg. "How are you feeling about the new job on Monday?"

He frowned. "I'm mostly excited. A little nervous too, though. This is the best chance I've had since I qualified. Even if it's only a temp job, it's in a good firm, and I'd love to work for them permanently if I get the chance. But that means I have more to lose. What if I'm crap at it or make a terrible first impression?"

"You won't be crap," Fiona assured him. "You're bright, you're capable, and you're not scared of hard work. You'll be great." Then her brow furrowed critically. "Although you might want to try and find a way of covering up the teeth marks on your neck, unless they've faded by Monday."

Ed flushed and reached up, touching the mark. It was tender under his fingertips. His cock stirred as he remembered the sounds Alec had made as they rocked together. "Yeah. Do you have some magic make-up I can use?"

"If you need it, but it probably won't be that noticeable by then." She grinned. "Now you have a respectable job, you'll need to tell your hook-ups to keep the marks below collar level."

"No more hook-ups." Ed hacked viciously into his bacon, accidentally shoving some baked beans off the edge of his plate. "I doubt I'll have time for any sort of love life for a while. I expect to be constantly exhausted and stressed out. It will just be me and my trusty right hand for the foreseeable future. Or maybe my left if I need variety."

On Sunday, Ed spent most of the day reading up on the law firm he was about to join. He surfed their website obsessively and reread all the information they'd sent him.

Late afternoon, he went to the gym and ran off some of his nervous energy on the treadmill before beating the hell out of a punchbag until his arms felt like jelly. Alec popped into his thoughts while he was working some of his stress out. The memory of Alec's coldness in the morning and the way he'd dismissed Ed made him punch the bag that much harder. He was pissed off with himself as much as Alec, angry that he'd let Alec get under his skin. What did it matter what a stranger thought of him, anyway? It had been a good fuck. That was all.

This evening was Ed's turn to cook, so he rustled up some pasta for them both. Fiona tried to tempt him with a glass of wine, suggesting it might help him to relax — "chill the fuck out" were her exact words — but Ed refused, not wanting to do anything that might compromise his alertness in the morning.

After dinner he was horribly anxious and couldn't settle to anything. He went to his room and pulled shirts and ties out of his wardrobe, rejecting each combination. At least he had a half-decent suit, thanks to a loan from his mum and stepdad. Once he got his first month's wages, he could pay them back and go shopping for some better work clothes.

Fiona tapped on his door.

"Come in."

"Need any help?" She came in and stood beside him.

"Will this do?" He gestured to the latest combination that he had lain out on the bottom of the bed.

"It's not bad, but do you have a tie with more blue in it?"

Ed rummaged around. "How about this one?"

"That's better." She nodded.

"Okay, thanks." Ed hung the selection on the back of his door ready for tomorrow morning.

"Now come and watch some TV with me and stop worrying. You're going to be brilliant." She slipped her arm through his and led him into the living room.

They watched a couple of old episodes of *Friends*, which was always a sure-fire way to make Ed laugh. Fiona got him to sit on the floor between her knees and massaged his shoulders until the muscles unknotted and some of his tension finally leaked away.

"Thanks." He tilted his head back to smile at her. "You're a star."

"I know." She grinned back and then yawned. "Okay, it's definitely my bedtime now. You should try and sleep too."

"Yes, Mum."

She ruffled his hair as he leaned forward to let her up. "Night, Ed."

Ed took his laptop to bed with him and checked his emails before attempting to settle down for the night. There was one from his mum, wishing him luck for tomorrow. She'd scanned in a picture the twins had drawn for him: balloons and flowers and assorted rabbits and birds in a variety of unlikely colours surrounded the words "Good luck Ed," written in giant bubble writing. He grinned as he admired it and then sent a copy to his printer so that he could stick it on his fridge along with other assorted pictures from the twins.

Fifteen years younger than Ed, eight-year-old Alice and Ava were the product of his mum's second marriage, along with his other half-sister, Gemma, who was fourteen.

Ed was close to his family and went home to visit them as often as he could. The seaside town of Worthing on the south coast was only about an hour and a half away from London, but fares were expensive and life was busy.

He typed in a quick reply to his mum, telling her to thank the twins for the picture and promising to try and visit soon.

Once he'd switched his lamp off, Ed ended up tossing and turning, unable to settle and get comfortable. His brain was in overdrive with all the stuff he'd been reading about his new job, and the anxious, churny feeling in his belly wasn't helping. He looked at the glowing red digits on his alarm clock and groaned when he saw it was well past midnight already. Ed tried to push the thoughts of tomorrow away and slow his breathing, forcing himself to relax. As his mind wandered he found himself thinking of Alec again, and inevitably those thoughts resulted in him getting hard.

Might as well, he thought as he slipped his hand into his pants and gave his cock a squeeze. A satisfying wank would probably help him sleep. He couldn't be bothered to power up his laptop again and look for some porn, so the memories of Alec would do nicely.

Ed closed his eyes and thought of hard muscles and dark chest hair. He ran his free hand over his nipples and remembered how Alec's chest had felt rubbing against his. He moved his hand faster over his prick, making sticky sounds. This wasn't going to take long. He rolled onto his side, fucking into his hand as he imagined Alec's cock between his thighs, his hands tight on Ed's hips as he bit down on Ed's neck.

"Fuck!" Ed came with a groan, making a total mess of his sheet in the process as he failed to catch much of it. "Bollocks," he muttered as his cock jerked again, and he squeezed out the last drops.

After he'd mopped up the wet patch with a couple of tissues, Ed collapsed and fell into a blissfully dreamless sleep.

CHAPTER THREE

Alec walked through the glass doors of Baker Wells into the lobby at seven thirty on Monday morning. They slid open as he passed through, out of the chill morning air and into the climate-controlled environment of the offices.

It was one of the largest and most prestigious law firms in London, but all was quiet at this time of day. Alec was usually one of the first into work. He enjoyed the peace and quiet and the time to organise his thoughts before the office filled with his colleagues. He was a creature of habit and tended to arrive at the same time every day, coffee that he had picked up from the Starbucks on the corner in one hand and his briefcase in the other.

He nodded good morning to the security guard and tapped his foot impatiently as he waited for the lift to take him up to the sixth floor. When the lift doors opened, Alec stepped out and padded quietly over plush carpets and along silent corridors until he reached the open-plan office space that he shared with his team. He took a seat at his desk, opened up his briefcase, peeled the protective lid carefully off his coffee—large, black, no sugar—and settled down to read through the files for the hotel deal they were currently working on.

Several months of legwork were finally coming to a head, but they still had a lot of details to iron out. The next few weeks would be crucial, hopefully leading to a deal that both parties would be happy with. A large national hotel chain, based in London, was in the process of buying up a smaller, but very successful, chain in Scotland.

Alec was the senior associate assigned to manage the deal. Although technically his boss, Katherine Parker, was in overall control and would oversee everything, Alec's role was running this deal. He was the one coordinating the team, leading the negotiations, and he would be drafting the main purchase agreement. There was still a lot of work to be done, and now the negotiations were picking up pace, two extra people were joining the team today. Alec hoped they'd pull their weight; they'd need to. One of them was a man from within the firm called Jon Kingsland, whom Alec knew but hadn't worked closely with before. He was a paralegal who had worked in Mergers and Acquisitions here at Baker Wells for a couple of years. The other was new, a recently qualified temp. Alec couldn't recall his name—he wasn't sure anyone had told him what it was yet. He hoped he wasn't too wet behind the ears and would manage to make himself useful. They didn't have time to babysit.

"Good morning, Alec. Putting the rest of us to shame as usual, I see." James Morgan, Associate, greeted Alec with a grin as he took his seat at his desk across the way.

Alec had worked with James for almost a year now, and they had a good working relationship. He appreciated James's humour and camaraderie as much as he did his attention to detail and his ability to smooth things out with even the most difficult clients.

"Did you have a good weekend?" James asked. "I hope you didn't spend the whole time working. I always worry when you email me at midnight on a Saturday."

Alec's lips quirked. "It was okay, thanks. And no, I didn't spend the whole time working. I do have a life, you know." A vision of Ed with his lips wrapped around Alec's cock popped unbidden into his head. He snapped the mental doors closed on it promptly. "My mother was in town, so I met her for lunch on Saturday."

After asking Ed to leave, Alec had breakfasted alone in his flat. He'd felt guilty lying to Ed to make him leave, but he wasn't enough of a bastard to throw Ed out without at least making some excuse. From the look on Ed's face, Alec didn't think he'd fooled him. But really, it served him right for falling asleep in a stranger's bed. Alec could have been an axe murderer or something. He found Ed's level of trust in him astonishing.

Damn it. Now he was thinking about Ed again, having spent most of the weekend trying to forget him. This was why he never let anyone stay the night after picking them up. Having someone sleep in his bed had unsettled Alec; his tightly guarded privacy had been invaded, and he felt uncomfortable.

"How about you?" Alec turned the question back to James. "Good weekend?"

"Not bad, thanks. It was Emily's birthday on Saturday, so we got a babysitter for Charlotte and I took Em out to dinner. Then I had a duty visit to the parents for Sunday lunch. Seems to have been the weekend for it."

Alec chuckled and turned his attention back to the papers spread out on his desk. He sipped at his coffee as he thought about his mother. "Duty" just about summed it up. Alec had always been the dutiful son.

He'd never had an easy relationship with either of his parents, but his mother was the lesser of two evils. His parents lived in the Berkshire countryside, near Newbury, and his mother visited London often for shopping and socialising. Alec was always expected to make time in his schedule to meet her when she was in town.

The rustle of paper indicated that James was settling down to work too, and they got on with things in silence as the office gradually filled up around them. The rest of the team greeted them as they arrived one by one and started getting themselves organised for the day. Once the new additions joined them a little later, there would be a meeting to make sure everyone was up to speed with the details of the takeover.

Alec lost himself in paperwork for a while, rereading some reports and making a few notes in the margins until Jen, the PA he shared with Katherine, interrupted him.

"Alec, the new temp is down in reception." Jen stood by his desk. "I'm just on my way down to meet him."

"Thanks, Jen. Bring him straight up. Then give him a quick tour before we meet at nine thirty to discuss the deal."

"Will do." Jen turned with a swish of her dark hair and hurried off.

Alec carried on reading. He was so focused on his task that he didn't notice the sound of footsteps approaching a little later.

"Alec."

Jen's voice made him raise his head. He looked at her first, before he let his gaze move to the man beside her. The polite smile froze on his face and adrenaline flooded his system with a jolt that nearly took his breath away.

"This is Ed Piper, your new trainee. Ed, this is Alec Rowland, Senior Associate. He's leading the team you'll be working with."

Ed barely reacted. There was the tiniest flare of anxiety in his eyes, but Alec only saw it because he was looking for it.

Alec stood to greet him, good breeding and thirty-two years of ingrained etiquette making his limbs move on autopilot. "Hello, Ed." He held out his hand.

"Hello, Mr Rowland," Ed said smoothly, taking Alec's proffered hand in his own.

"Alec, please. We use first names here. It's good to meet you," he replied without a flicker of irony. But his palm was clammy in Ed's warm grip and his gaze dropped from the clear blue of Ed's eyes to his pink lips, which were parted in an uncertain smile. Alec swallowed hard and dragged his gaze back up to meet Ed's. "Welcome to the team." He dropped Ed's hand as though it were on fire and cleared his throat, turning back to his desk.

Oblivious, Jen guided Ed away to introduce him to the rest of their colleagues, leaving Alec stunned. He collapsed gratefully into his chair, legs shaking as his heart pounded.

The meeting was excruciating.

Alec was distracted and furious with himself for being so unsettled by Ed's presence. He was normally never less than 100 percent professional, utterly focused on his work. But having Ed sitting there was driving him crazy.

Ed didn't display any outward signs of discomfort. He listened attentively, taking a few notes as Alec outlined the progress that had been made so far on the deal, and explained what still needed to be done. Alec was painfully aware of Ed watching him as he spoke and tried to avoid his gaze as much as he could, without making it obvious he was doing so.

He wondered what the fuck Ed was thinking. Surely he must be rattled too? Nobody liked their private life being dragged into the workplace. He was going to need to speak to Ed alone. Alec had so much to lose; he had to make sure Ed could be discreet.

"Thank you, Alec," Katherine said. "Does anyone have any questions before we move on to the financial reports?" She looked around the table. "No? Okay. Over to you, then, Maria. Can you fill us in on the state of Mackenzie's finances?"

Alec relaxed a little and let his attention wander as Maria Ortega took over. Until Jon had joined them this morning, she had been the only paralegal on the team. Five foot nothing but with a huge personality that made her seem larger, Maria was great at her job. Alec had read through her findings over the weekend, so he knew what she'd be saying and could get away with letting his mind wander. He half-listened to her lilting Spanish accent as she outlined the key points to bring the rest of the team up to speed. But his mind was busy mulling over the situation with Ed and wondering what Ed might be thinking about it all.

Alec chanced a glance at Ed, who was sitting adjacent to him, his back to the window. Alec stiffened as he noticed a fading purple bruise on the skin of Ed's neck. Alec's heart rate soared as a vivid sense memory—the salt of Ed's skin under his tongue, the scent of his sweat, and the heat of their bodies moving together—assaulted him. Alec's cock tingled and thickened in his underwear, and he forced himself to look away. A quick glance around the table reassured him that everyone's attention was on Maria and his personal crisis was going unnoticed.

Unable to help himself, Alec let his gaze slide back to Ed's neck. The mark was barely noticeable, and if he hadn't been the one responsible for it, he probably wouldn't have even realised what it was. Only part of it showed above Ed's collar, and Alec found himself longing to see it all, to see what other marks he'd left on that smooth skin.

Ed turned his head then, and his gaze locked on Alec's for a couple of uncomfortable seconds before Alec looked away.

Sweat prickled on Alec's back, and his heart pounded as though he'd been sprinting. He needed to get a fucking grip, and he needed to talk to Ed alone as soon as possible. Alec couldn't deal with this kind of distraction at work; he had a job to do.

Unfortunately for Alec, open-plan offices didn't provide much opportunity for private conversations, and he couldn't whisk Ed off to one of the small breakout rooms they used for meetings without it looking suspicious.

Alec did his best to ignore Ed throughout the morning. He buried himself in his work and gave James the job of babysitting Ed and finding him some dogsbody jobs to do—hopefully ones that would keep him occupied and away from Alec as much as possible.

There were piles of paperwork Ed was required to sort and relevant sections that needed copying and distributing to the team. Ed settled down to the tasks without any fuss and seemed to be getting through them all efficiently. The desk Ed had been allocated had its back to Alec's, and Alec did his best not to be distracted by the nape of Ed's neck and the way his dark blond hair grew down into a point at the back.

The sound of a throat clearing drew Alec's attention away from his laptop screen.

"Sorry to disturb you, Alec." Ed's voice was formal. "But can you remind me where the photocopier is, please? Jen showed me earlier, but my sense of direction is terrible."

Alec cast his gaze around. James was at his desk across the way, talking on the phone, and Jon and Maria were nowhere to be seen. Alec wasn't going to risk having the conversation he needed to have here, where they could potentially be overheard. "Yeah, sure," he replied curtly. "It's down the corridor, third door on the left."

"Thanks." Ed forced a little half smile. He hesitated for a moment before speaking in a quiet rush. "I'm not going to say anything, you know." His gaze was open and honest, and Alec could see something there that looked infuriatingly like compassion.

"Not now," Alec hissed. He knew his voice sounded like ice, but he needed Ed to shut the hell up. "We'll talk later."

Ed nodded, cheeks flushing bright pink, and he gave a tiny jerk of his head in assent. "Okay."

Alec watched him as he walked away. Ed had taken off his suit jacket, and his arse looked just as delicious as Alec remembered.

He closed his eyes. He was so fucked.

At lunchtime, Jen phoned in a sandwich order to the deli that was popular with the people in their office. She went round the team, checking what they wanted. Alec ordered his usual chicken and avocado even though he wasn't feeling particularly hungry. His nerves and preoccupation at the sudden and unexpected appearance of Ed in his workplace had killed his appetite.

"Do you want anything, Ed?" Jen asked when she got to his desk.

"No thanks. I brought my own lunch today. I wasn't sure what to expect."

"I usually bring mine too." Alec glanced up to see Jen smiling reassuringly at Ed. "The deli's lovely, but it's not exactly cheap."

"I can imagine," Ed replied.

When Jen came back with their order, they ate at their desks as usual. Getting crumbs on laptops was an occupational hazard, but Alec never saw the point in taking a proper break at lunchtime. He worked long enough hours as it was without wasting half an hour in the middle of the day. The rest of the team seemed to feel the same, because nobody ever complained.

When he finished eating, Alec was hit by the urge for some post-lunch caffeine. Coffee and tea making and fetching was traditionally the job of the newest minion on the team. Normally Alec wouldn't have thought twice about asking a temp to fetch him coffee but he felt oddly uncomfortable about bossing Ed around. He was going to need to get past that, and there was no time like the present.

"Hey, Ed." Alec's voice came out sounding a little forced, full of over-the-top bravado. He toned it down, trying to sound casual as Ed turned his head to look at him expectantly. "Any chance of a round of coffees? It might not be in your job description, but traditionally the buck stops with the newbie."

"Oh, of course. There's a machine in the kitchen, isn't there? Or do you need me to go out for them?"

"From the machine is fine."

"Okay." Ed stood and grabbed a pen and a Post-it note. "You'd better place your orders, then."

Alec followed Ed with his gaze as Ed took orders from each of the team in turn. Katherine's office door was closed and she was deep in conversation on her phone. Ed hesitated, obviously wondering whether to knock or not.

"Don't disturb her." Alec warned him. "She'll have tea, white, no sugar. Make sure you use skimmed milk."

"Thanks, will do."

Ed's sudden smile made him look ridiculously young. Alec remembered how Ed had looked in the club the first time he'd seen him, that grin lighting up his face and drawing Alec in like a magnet. He suppressed the instinctive urge to smile back, just nodding slightly before turning back to his desk.

Alec was on his way back from a meeting with the guys in Real Estate when he took a detour to the bathroom. The sight of a familiar figure at the urinals sent a jolt of nerves through him. This might not be the ideal place to talk, but they were currently alone and it was the best chance he'd had all day without anyone overhearing them.

He shifted his weight uncomfortably from foot to foot. Luckily, Ed was finishing, zipping himself back up, so Alec didn't have to wait like a creepy lurker for long. "Hi," he said as Ed turned around and saw him standing there, just inside the closed door that led out to the corridor.

"Am I allowed to talk to you now?" Ed's voice had an edge to it as he walked over to the sinks and started washing his hands. He met Alec's gaze in the mirrors, his blue eyes challenging.

"I don't think having this conversation in our office space would be in either of our best interests, do you?" Alec clenched his fist in his pocket, irritated by Ed's attitude, by his very presence that threatened Alec's orderly existence.

Ed shook the water off his hands and used a paper towel to dry them. "Well, you'd better make it quick." He balled the towel up and threw it into the bin with perfect aim. He turned and leaned back against the sinks, arms folded, waiting.

Alec bit down on his rising annoyance, determined not to give Ed the upper hand in this situation. "I just wanted to make sure you realise it would be a very bad idea to let anyone know about what happened on Friday night." He gritted his teeth, willing himself not to flush as he alluded to their night together.

Ed's cheeks were pink and his eyes glittered in the bright spotlights that were positioned in the ceiling. "I already told you I wouldn't," he said tightly. "I'm not completely stupid. I want to focus on work and do my job. I'm hardly going to go around bragging that I've fucked my new boss."

His words made bright anger pour through Alec, and heat flooded his face and neck. He opened his mouth to retort, but Ed spoke again before he could find the words.

"Look. I don't want anyone to know either. Not because I'm ashamed of my sexuality, but our little encounter on Friday night doesn't make for a fun anecdote that I'll be sharing with my new colleagues. I'm a professional, and I'm planning on behaving like one."

"Good. I'm glad we're on the same page." Alec relaxed a little at Ed's assurances.

"I presume you're not out at work, then?" Ed raised his eyebrows.

"I'm not out full stop." Alec met Ed's blue gaze and saw it soften, almost imperceptibly.

Ed paused for a moment before he spoke again. "That sounds lonely. But don't worry. I'm not going to out you."

Somehow Alec knew he could trust him. He nodded and swallowed around a lump that had appeared in his throat. "Thanks."

"But just so you know, I'm not planning on pretending to be anything I'm not. People often assume anyway." Ed shrugged. "I'm not very good at flying under people's gaydar."

Alec's lips quirked. "I can imagine." There was a flamboyance to Ed, a brightness he didn't try to hide.

"These days, when it comes up, I tell people. I prefer to be upfront about it. I wouldn't have minded being in the closet at school, but it wasn't really an option." The tone in Ed's voice made it clear he wasn't joking.

"They gave you a hard time?"

"You could say that."

There was a long silence. Alec wanted to ask Ed to elaborate, but this wasn't the time or the place for a lengthy conversation. He knew from his own experiences at school how ruthless kids could be in making life miserable for anyone they perceived as different. Alec had escaped that himself. He had fit the masculine stereotype, and it was easy to pretend to be fascinated by girls, when in an all-boys boarding school, he naturally had very little contact with the opposite sex. He remembered how it had been for boys who had drawn unwanted attention by being gender non-conforming. The irony was that most of the boys who were teased for being queer at school were probably straight. Outward appearances were frequently deceptive, and half the boys doing the teasing weren't averse to a bit of mutual masturbation on occasion, whatever their sexuality. All those teenage hormones made for a melting pot of sexual confusion.

"You should get back to your desk." Alec hadn't intended for it to come out as a dismissal, but the shutters came down on Ed's face immediately, and the brief moment of connection they'd shared was over.

"Of course." Ed straightened up from his position against the sinks and moved towards the door.

When he reached it, Alec called after him. "Ed?" Ed turned. "Thanks."

Ed nodded in acknowledgement, and then he pulled the door open and was gone.

Alec was sitting at his desk.

The rest of Alec's team had packed up and gone home. Ed had been among the last to leave, staying until nearly half past eight to finish the filing James had given him to do.

He'd left with a wave and a tentative smile. "See you in the morning."

Alec had raised a hand and made himself smile back.

He sighed and rubbed his temples, the familiar ache indicating he'd overdone the screen time. He saved and closed the document he was working on, shut down his laptop, and then started to pack away the things he needed to finish this evening from home.

Alec *was* lonely.

Loneliness was such a fundamental fact of his life that Alec rarely paid attention to it anymore. But ever since the conversation with Ed earlier, in the bathroom, Ed's words kept replaying in his head on a loop: *That sounds lonely.*

Alec had good relationships with his colleagues, just as with the friends he had socialised with at university. Yet hiding a significant part of himself meant he inevitably kept people at a distance. It was hard to develop any sort of close friendship while constantly worrying about giving away his secret.

Usually it didn't bother him that he was so emotionally isolated. He'd had a challenging relationship with both his parents at the best of times. He'd never been particularly close to his younger brother, Caspar, either. Despite being only two years apart in age, they were very different in temperaments and interests. Caspar had been the wild rebel, whereas Alec had always tried to toe the line.

Alec leaned wearily against the wall of the lift as it descended to the ground floor, lost in unhappy memories.

Desperate to please his demanding father, Alec had worked hard at school and achieved what was expected of him. But it had all fallen apart in his final year at school on the day his housemaster had gone on the prowl looking for boys smoking illicit cigarettes in the shrubbery. He got more than he bargained for when he found Alec getting sucked off by Harris, one of the fifth-formers, a pretty boy with long eyelashes and a mouth like a vacuum cleaner.

Unfortunately for Alec and Harris, their public school — one of the top five in England — had been working hard to clean up its reputation after an old boy had published a scandalous memoir the year before. Prior to that unfortunate publicity, they might have got away with a stern warning. But now the game had changed. The headmaster was informed, their parents were called, and both boys were expelled immediately.

The fallout had been ugly. Alec preferred not to remember the hour he'd spent in his father's study the day his parents brought him home. He still carried the scars from it—on his skin as well as in his psyche—and thinking about it still made him nauseous.

He'd only had a few months to go until his A levels, and he'd already had an unconditional offer from Oxford. Rather than sending him to another school halfway through the year, his father had kept him at home with a tutor. Alec suspected it was so that his parents could keep an eye on him.

Alec's already difficult relationship with his parents had become intolerable during those few months. His father's disappointment and obvious disgust was hard for Alec to bear, and his mother had hovered on the edges of their antagonism, trying not to get involved. Eventually, Alec managed to convince his father it meant nothing—it was only a bit of youthful, hormone-driven stupidity.

I'm not gay.

Everyone knew things like that happened at public school. Alec's only mistake was getting caught.

Afterwards, Alec made damn sure he never got caught again.

He stepped out into the cold evening air and breathed in deeply. The scent of city streets and car exhaust made him long for the clean air of the countryside. Maybe once he'd closed this deal, he could have a weekend away in a place where buildings didn't block the sky.

CHAPTER FOUR

"So, how did it go?" Fiona asked as soon as Ed got through the door of their flat.

"Uh. Okay... sort of." Ed didn't even stop to take his coat and shoes off before collapsing on the sofa in the living room. He paused to gather his thoughts, and Fiona spoke again before he could elaborate.

"I made some soup, there's enough for you if you want?"

"Oh God, yes please." Ed's stomach growled at the thought of food, and he realised it was about eight hours since he'd eaten lunch.

Fiona studied him, a mixture of sympathy and amusement on her face. "You look knackered. I'll heat some up for you while you get out of that suit, then you can tell me about your day."

Five minutes later, Ed had curled up on the sofa again, dressed in slobbing-around-at-home clothes with a hot mug of soup and toasted cheese sandwiches.

"You're an actual angel," he told Fiona. "Thank you."

"You're welcome. Now, tell me what it was like. I want to know everything."

"Well... it was what you'd expect. Swanky offices, terrifyingly efficient people everywhere. But it was amazing too. I'm so excited just about being there, about being part of the organisation. This is what I've always wanted. I still can't believe I'm doing it." Ed paused to sip his soup. He was deliberately saving the best of his story till last. Ed couldn't resist spinning it out for maximum drama. If his life was going to be a soap opera—and apparently it was turning out that way—then he was damn well going to enjoy spilling the juicy details.

"And your boss?" Fiona asked.

"Yeah, about him…." Ed side-eyed her and felt the curl of his lips give him away. He had no idea why he was laughing. It wasn't funny. It was a fucking nightmare, to be honest, but he had to laugh about it—because crying wasn't going to help. "Remember the guy I fucked on Friday night?"

She frowned. "Mr Tall, Dark, and Sexy? Sure, I remember—" The light dawned and her expression turned from confusion to half horror, half glee. "Nooooo!" She covered her mouth with her hands, eyebrows shooting up to her hairline.

"Yep."

"Oh my God. Oh. My. *God*!"

Ed nodded. That pretty much summed up his thoughts on it. He'd been reeling ever since he first clapped eyes on Alec that morning. What were the chances? Of all the guys in London he could have picked up, it had to be his new boss.

"Did he recognise you? Did he say anything? Holy fuck, this is huge! Are you okay?"

"Yes, of course he recognised me!" Ed said, offended. "He ignored me all day, and then he got me alone in the toilets and warned me not to say anything to anyone—like I would. But I think he's as freaked out as I am, maybe even more because he's in the closet. I actually felt a little sorry for him, even though he was a bit of an arsehole about it."

"Wow. Is he married or what?"

Ed's stomach lurched. He hadn't even considered that. "I don't think so?" Alec's flat had looked like the home of a bachelor, and unlike James, Alec had no photos on his desk of a wife and children. "No. I'm pretty sure he isn't. But he's definitely not out, at work or anywhere. He told me."

"So with you showing up, he must be shitting himself."

"Yeah, exactly. So anyway, I told him I wouldn't say anything, and he seemed to relax a little. But it's going to be very weird working with him with that hanging over us."

"And you liked him too."

Fiona cut right to the heart of Ed's dilemma. Because despite everything, he couldn't help feeling drawn to Alec. They'd been such a good fit sexually. His body responded to Alec even when his brain told him it was a terrible idea. And during the conversation in the toilets, he'd seen a flash of vulnerability in Alec that only made him more appealing. The chink in Alec's armour had showed Ed a hint of a lonely man, and it made Ed want to get closer to him. If things were different, he'd probably be tempted to try.

"Yeah, well. He's my boss now, so I'll have to let that go. This job is my priority."

Ed's first week at Baker Wells flew by in a blur. The learning curve was like scaling Everest, but it was thrilling to be working at such a prestigious firm. Alongside the mundane duties of filing, copying, and coffee making that fell to him as the newest on the team, Ed also had to read vast quantities of paperwork to get him up to speed with the deal the team was working on.

He worked twelve-or-more-hour days alongside the rest of the team and barely had the energy to do anything other than shower, eat, and sleep when he was at home. He tried watching TV with Fiona in the evening a couple of times, but inevitably dozed off within a few minutes of sitting still.

The atmosphere between him and Alec still felt tense to Ed, but nobody else in the team seemed to pick up on it. Their interactions were strictly work related, and every time Alec spoke to him, Ed's heart rate picked up a notch, and when he caught Alec's piercing gaze on him, it made the back of his neck prickle with heat. Alec was so bloody attractive, and having known him in the biblical sense, it was very hard to see him as just a colleague now. Ed's traitorous libido wanted more.

By late afternoon on Friday, Ed was light-headed with exhaustion. He was sitting at his desk, supposedly proofreading a letter that needed to go out on Monday, but his eyes kept glazing over. Ed dragged his gaze up to the window and stared at the darkening sky. He left home in the mornings before it was light, and he got home in darkness too. Thank goodness the office had large windows. But he missed getting outdoors in daylight hours.

"You nearly done there, Ed?" James called across from his desk. He was the one who had given Ed the letter to check.

"Yes, sorry." Ed snapped his attention back to the screen. His eyes were dry and he rubbed them, blinking, trying to wake himself up.

A few minutes later, he was done. "I've emailed it back to you. There were just a couple of queries."

"Thanks." James smiled. "You coming out for a drink tonight? It's a Friday tradition to pop down to the wine bar on the corner before we head home for the weekend. It's good for team bonding."

"Oh, um. I'm not sure." Ed had been looking forward to getting home and falling asleep on the sofa while he watched Friday-night TV. The thought of having to keep up his workplace persona for an extra hour or so was far from appealing. His colleagues had been very welcoming—apart from Alec—but Ed felt as though he constantly had to be on his best behaviour in front of them.

"Go on. Everyone comes... even Alec, who spends most of his life chained to his desk. Although I have a sneaking suspicion he just goes home to do more work afterwards."

Ed glanced at Alec, who was listening in to the conversation. *Not every Friday he doesn't*, he thought.

Alec's cheeks tinged with pink as though he knew what was going through Ed's mind. He cleared his throat and said, "Yes, you should come, Ed. The first round's on me."

Ed couldn't decline now without looking churlish. Maybe spending more time around Alec would help to ease the awkwardness between them.

The bar was all chrome, glass, and black leather, combined with slightly cold lighting that made it feel clinical rather than cosy. The prices on the menu made Ed double-take. He'd been living in London long enough that he shouldn't be surprised by now, but he was used to cheaper student haunts with happy hours and special offers on pitchers. This place was a far cry from that.

Alec didn't bat an eyelid as the team placed their orders with the cute waiter. Several of them went for cocktails, and tempting though it was to ask for a Slow Comfortable Screw to see if he could make Alec blush, Ed repressed his instinct for mischief. It was only after he'd requested a rum and Coke that he remembered it was what Alec had bought for him almost exactly a week ago. A flash of recognition in Alec's eyes told Ed that he hadn't forgotten either.

"Do you want a double?" Alec's face was impassive as he added, "I think you've earned one this week."

Disarmed, Ed smiled. "Yes. Thank you." A warm glow crept through him at Alec's approval.

"Yes, you've done well." James clapped Ed on the shoulder, and several of the others chipped in, agreeing.

Ed flushed, unable to hide his pleasure at the praise. "I'm glad you think so. Thanks, guys."

The waiter left the table.

"So Ed," James said, "tell me a bit about yourself. How did you end up temping at Baker Wells?"

"I'm actually looking for something permanent in employment law eventually," Ed admitted, looking nervously at Alec, who was watching him as he spoke. Maybe it wasn't wise to confess that his true interests didn't lie in corporate. "But at the moment I'll take any experience I can get."

James carried on quizzing Ed about his education and then about his family. The rest of the group split off into their own conversations, distracted only by the arrival of their drinks. Alec was sitting opposite, talking with Maria, but Ed was aware of him glancing in his direction occasionally and was sure Alec was only half listening to Maria.

James was open and friendly, chatting proudly about his daughter, Charlotte. He showed Ed some photos on his phone of a smiling toddler with wispy curls, so Ed showed James a picture of his sisters that he'd taken last summer on the beach in Worthing.

The waiter came back to take orders for a second round of drinks, but Ed still had some left, so he declined. He noticed Alec had drunk his first glass of red rather quickly.

"So, are you young free and single, Ed? Or do you have a girl to get home to tonight?" James asked.

Ed glanced across at Alec. Maria was talking, but the lines of Alec's body were tense, and Ed knew Alec had heard James's question and was listening for Ed's reply. "The only girl at home is my housemate, but we're just friends." Ed paused and then decided he wouldn't get a better opportunity to mention his sexuality. "Actually, if I were dating someone, it would be a guy, not a girl, but there's nobody at the moment. Probably for the best, I don't have the energy for anything outside work right now."

Ed registered James's reaction—not surprise, exactly, but a quick mental shift of gears. He covered it well. "Yeah. This job doesn't make a private life easy," he agreed. "Emily's always complaining she never sees enough of me."

Ed chanced another look at Alec. He was smiling at something Maria had said. As Ed watched, Alec's gaze flashed to Ed, and their eyes met for a second. Something there told Ed he was right. Alec had definitely overheard his conversation with James.

"Speaking of which," James continued, "I'd better head home. It's my turn to get up with Charlotte in the morning—she's an early riser and I promised Emily a lie-in tomorrow." He drained the last of his drink. "Night everyone, have a good weekend. Don't spend too much of it working."

Once James had gone, the others began to make their excuses and drift off. Soon it was only Alec, Ed, and Maria left. Ed was still nursing his first drink, but it was almost empty now. He needed the toilet, so made his excuses and left Alec and Maria together. When he returned, Maria had her coat on and was wrapping a scarf around her neck.

She smiled at Ed. "I'm sorry, I have to go and catch my bus. But you can stay and keep Alec company." Alec still had half a glass of red wine in front of him. "Bye. I'll see you both on Monday."

Ed slid back into his seat, picking up his drink and swirling it so the ice cubes clinked against the glass. The liquid in it was mostly iced water now, but he sipped it anyway for something to do.

"Well, this is weird." He raised his gaze to meet Alec's in a challenge. Ed was tired of pretending. There was no need to keep up the polite facade now the others had gone.

"Is it?" Alec's posture was relaxed, but Ed wondered whether it was genuine. He curled his long fingers around the stem of his wine glass and slid them up and down in a way that drew Ed's eyes and inevitably sent his mind to dirty places. Alec lifted the glass and took a careful sip. "It didn't take you long to come out at work, did it? Nicely done. And James is the sort to mention it, so word will get around. I assume that was your intention."

"Yes. Quick and painless. The sooner it's common knowledge, the better. James didn't seem bothered."

"Of course he wasn't." Alec's voice was brusque. "People have more important things to worry about than who you like to fuck."

Ed raised his eyebrows. "So, how come you're in the closet, then?"

There was a flicker of anger on Alec's face, and Ed wondered whether he'd gone too far. He looked at the ice cubes in his drink again. Their sharp corners had melted away into smoothness. If only the jagged edges of his relationship with Alec could be softened so easily.

Ed assumed he wasn't going to get an answer, so he was surprised when Alec finally spoke.

"Years of habit." Alec sounded weary rather than irritated. "I've been lying to people for a long time, by omission at the very least. Coming out in your first week at a new job is probably easy in comparison—not that I'd know—but it's not something I could just drop casually into conversation now. It would be the equivalent of tossing a hand grenade into the room. I'd lose my integrity because people would know I'd deliberately deceived them."

"How?"

"Ask anyone at the office, and they'll tell you I have a girlfriend."

Ed felt a lurch of nausea. He didn't like to think Alec had cheated on someone with him, but he also hated imagining Alec with anyone else, which was ridiculous. "And do you?"

"Not in the way they think." Alec sighed. "She's called Belinda. She's an old friend from Oxford, and she's more than happy to pretend to be a casual girlfriend for social occasions — especially ones involving free alcohol and nice restaurants."

"Handy." Ed kept his voice light.

"So you see, coming out would be a little more complicated for me than it was for you."

"I suppose." Ed wanted to know more about why Alec was so deeply closeted in the first place, but he sensed Alec would clam up if he tried to dig. The wine seemed to have loosened his tongue a little, yet only within careful limits.

"You turning up on Monday morning was the last thing I needed."

"I'm sorry to be such an inconvenience." Ed tried to make it sound like a joke, but his throat was dry and it came out tight and awkward. "It's not a barrel of laughs for me either, you know." He met Alec's gaze. Alec's hazel eyes were almost luminous with the way the light caught them. Ed felt pinned, unable to look away despite his rising discomfort as Alec stared at him.

"Maybe if we fuck each other again, we can get it out of our systems?" Alec suggested.

His tone was so conversational that it took a moment for Ed to register what he'd said, but then his heart surged and all the blood in his body redistributed itself in a lightning bolt of arousal. He blinked, wondering whether he'd really heard Alec right. The words replayed in his head on a loop. "You have to be kidding me."

Alec wasn't smiling. "I'm deadly serious." His poker face was impressive.

Ed studied him, desperately hoping his own emotional turmoil wasn't obvious. He searched for a chink in that impassivity, trying to work out what the fuck Alec was thinking, but there was nothing there to give him a clue. "What on earth makes you think it would be a good idea to go down that road again?"

"Who said it was a good idea?" Alec's lips twitched, finally betraying something, although amusement wasn't what Ed had been expecting.

He found himself responding against his better judgement, a smile tugging at his mouth as he replied. "Typical bloody lawyer."

Alec grinned properly then, and Ed realised it was the first time he'd seen Alec with his guard down. He was so beautiful when he smiled that it made Ed's chest ache with wanting to see it more often.

"Okay." Alec held up his hand, ticking his arguments off on his fingers as he spoke. "We're both adults, we already know we're sexually compatible, you've shown you can be discreet, and we've already done it once, so it's too late to worry about it."

"We've set a precedent, you mean?" Ed raised his eyebrows.

"Exactly. So, what do you say?"

"Who said I need to get you out of my system?" Ed asked, attempting nonchalance.

"Are you hard right now?" Alec's gaze bored into him.

Ed felt a shameful rush of heat rise from under his collar to the tips of his ears. He opened his mouth to deny it, but nothing came out.

"I rest my case."

Alec folded his arms, a smug grin stretching over his face, and Ed wanted to kiss it away with fierce, biting kisses. Ed stared at Alec as the seconds ticked by. He felt as though he was poised on the edge of a cliff ready to dive. The water below beckoned, luring him down, but who knew what rocks or monsters lay below the surface? The fall might be exhilarating, but Ed wasn't sure he'd survive it.

Self-preservation won out over temptation. "No," he said firmly. "There's no way it could end well."

A muscle clenched in Alec's jaw but he held Ed's gaze. "I'm not looking for a happy ending," he said lightly. "Just a mutual relief of tension. It would make a nice change from finding a stranger to fuck." Something in the tone of his voice made Ed feel an odd rush of pity. How lonely must Alec be to ask this of Ed?

Ed shook his head, trying to stay strong. "It would be way too complicated." His feelings about Alec were already a clusterfuck of confusion. The last thing he needed was to add to it by fucking

Alec again. "I think it would be better to keep our relationship strictly professional."

Alec's jaw tightened, but whether it was with anger or disappointment, Ed couldn't tell. "You're probably right." Alec sounded defeated. He looked away from Ed, down at the glass in his hand.

Ed almost wished Alec hadn't given up trying to persuade him so soon. If he'd been a little more persistent, he might have been impossible to resist.

"I'm sorry," Ed said softly. Without thinking about what he was doing, he reached across the table and touched the back of Alec's hand, his fingertips grazing the dark hairs that dusted it.

Alec snatched his hand away, glancing around to make sure nobody was paying them any attention. "It's fine." His voice was acid, and two patches of colour burned on his cheeks. "Don't flatter yourself, Mr Piper. Your arse isn't that special. I simply thought it might be convenient. My mistake." He picked up his wine glass and drained the contents before standing and pulling on his coat. "I'll see you on Monday morning. Goodbye."

Ed watched as Alec stalked away, his broad shoulders military straight. The door swung shut behind him, and he was gone.

Suddenly overcome with exhaustion, Ed let his head droop. He stared at the rings of condensation that his drink had left on the glass table. "Fuck," he muttered. Had he messed up his chances of succeeding at this job before he'd even got started? He hadn't done anything wrong, but working with Alec might prove impossible. Maybe he could ask for a transfer to a different team…. But he couldn't do that without an explanation, and they might not need a temp anywhere else. No, he was just going to have to keep his head down, get through the next few weeks, and avoid Alec as much as he could.

CHAPTER FIVE

Alec hesitated in the street, debating hailing a cab. His whole body was aflame with humiliation and anger. He put his head back and stared into the murky darkness of the city sky. The air was freezing, and a few tiny flakes of sleet stung his face. He took a deep breath and exhaled a muttered, "Fuck." He felt a little better, so he did it again, louder this time. "Fucking, *fuck*!"

He set off on foot. If he got tired of walking, he could grab a cab a little closer to home, but this way he might stand a chance of burning off some of the irrational fury boiling in his veins.

The anger was directed at himself, not Ed. How could he have been so stupid? Even if Ed had said yes, it would have been a disaster. Alec had spent years keeping his private life utterly separate from his work. It would be madness to change that now. Thank fuck Ed had his head screwed on, because Alec appeared to be thinking with an organ a few degrees south of his brain.

Arriving at the corner, he paused. One way would take him into the darker streets towards home, the other led towards the bright lights of a district where there were plenty of gay bars and clubs. Places where Alec knew he could click his fingers and get laid ten times over if he wanted. He needed something to try and obliterate thoughts of Ed, to erase this temporary insanity that surged through him like a fever.

The decision made, he turned away from home.

Half an hour later, he was still nursing a single shot of whisky and had lost count of the offers he'd turned down. He was normally fairly choosy, but this was ridiculous, even for him.

There was nothing objectively wrong with any of the guys who'd tried to get his attention tonight, other than the fact that they weren't Ed. Yet none of them raised even a tiny spark of interest, no matter how attractive they were. Alec was already mortified enough by his actions this evening without adding to it by failing to get it up while some pretty boy sucked his dick. Sighing, he drained his glass and shook his head at the latest twink to sidle up and try to catch his eye. The guy shrugged regretfully and moved on.

If only Alec could do the same with Ed.

The next week passed in a blur of paperwork, meetings, and mind-numbing exhaustion as Alec threw himself into his current project with even more manic energy than normal. He worked his usual long days, went to the gym most evenings after work, and passed out around midnight every night. Yet inappropriate thoughts of Ed still crept into his consciousness, and even into his dreams.

Still furious with himself for letting his guard down, Alec dealt with his anger by taking it out on Ed in the workplace. Always a hard taskmaster and critical of any weakness shown by graduate trainees, Alec was even more ruthless with Ed. He gave him seemingly impossible amounts of work:

piles of paperwork to sort and manage, agreements to draft and proof, contracts to review.

Ed rose to every challenge.

He was good; Alec had to admit that. Probably one of the best temps he'd seen in years, but he was damned if he was going to tell Ed. Instead, like the shoemaker in the old fairy story, he kept increasing Ed's workload, wanting to find the point where he'd break.

On Wednesday evening, James called him out on it.

Ed had worked late that day, not leaving till after seven. Then, just as he was putting on his coat to leave, Alec had given him another massive pile of paperwork to check.

"Sorry to land this on you so late, but could you get this back to me by eight tomorrow morning?" Always utterly courteous on the surface, Alec kept his voice smooth and polite. "I need it for a telephone meeting with the Scottish accountants."

"Of course." Ed did a good job of hiding his frustration, but Alec could read it in the tightness of his jaw as he took the pile of files. "Is it okay if I go through them at home?" He had violet shadows under his eyes and the day's dusting of stubble on his jaw. He looked like death warmed up, yet he still made Alec's stomach twist with an unsettling combination of longing and desire.

"Absolutely. As long as it gets done."

"Okay. See you in the morning."

Once he'd left, James said, "Don't you think you're pushing him a little hard?"

"He can handle it," Alec replied curtly. "And if he can't, then I'm doing him a favour. Better to know now so he can find another job. You know it will only get tougher."

"True. But it's only his second week."

"And we're supposed to be closing this deal in less than six. We can't afford to give anyone on this team an easy ride." Alec's tone brooked no argument and James backed off. Alec remembered those shadows under Ed's eyes and felt a twinge of guilt. He hoped Ed would manage to get at least a few hours of sleep tonight.

"What's everyone doing this weekend?" James asked as they sat around their usual table on Friday night.

Alec had been careful to sit well away from Ed. He didn't want a repeat of last week. One drink and then home, that was the plan.

"Sleeping," Ed said, lips quirking in a rueful grin. "In between going through the latest batch of figures Alec dumped on me an hour ago." He caught Alec's eye.

Alec shrugged. "Sleep is for the weak. Haven't you learned that yet?" But he smiled, chest tugging as Ed's grin widened.

"I think the last week has taught me sleep is a luxury, that's for sure."

"What about you, Maria? Do you have plans for anything more exciting than sleeping?" James asked.

"I'm having lunch with my brother and his boyfriend tomorrow—or rather, I should say his fiancé. They're getting married soon." Maria smiled, her brown eyes softening.

Alec caught Ed's gaze as everyone around the table chimed in with words of congratulation and started asking her about the wedding plans. He looked away from Ed quickly, trying to focus on what Maria was saying about winter weddings and venues. Longing swelled in his chest like a fist unclenching, and not for the first time he found himself questioning whether staying in the closet had been the right decision. He had success, money, respect… but what might his life be like if he had someone to share it with?

"Alec?" Maria put her hand on his arm, and the room came back into focus.

"What? Sorry, Maria, I was miles away."

"I was asking you what you're doing this weekend. All work, no play?" Her voice was deep for such a small woman.

"Depends what you count as work, I suppose," he replied. "I'm having dinner with Katherine and some of the other partners tomorrow, so it's somewhere between business and pleasure."

"Oho." James raised his glass. "Getting your feet under the table in anticipation?"

They all knew Alec was hoping to make partner this year. He'd been going through the application process for the past few months and would find out soon whether he'd been successful.

"Something like that." Alec smiled, refusing to be drawn. He already knew his chances were good, but this deal they were working on was crucial. Katherine may be supervising, but it was his baby. If the team pulled it off, Alec would win major brownie points and his promotion almost assured.

"Are you taking the lovely Belinda?" James grinned.

Despite being happily married, he had an embarrassingly obvious crush on her. Belinda tended to have that effect on most straight men. It was ironic, really, when Alec was totally immune, but it came in handy when trying to impress his male colleagues.

"Of course. Who else?"

"When are you going to make an honest woman of her? I can't believe she puts up with the hours you work when you don't even live together yet. She must hardly ever see you." James frowned. "You should put a ring on it before she kicks you to the kerb. Get her settled in that lovely flat of yours with a baby."

Alec suppressed a smile. Even if he had been dating Belinda, he could imagine how she'd respond to the suggestion of marriage, let alone having a family. Belinda was a free spirit when it came to relationships and utterly career driven. An interior designer who worked for the rich and famous, she was the only person Alec knew who worked as hard as he did — maybe harder.

"I don't think she's the settling-down type. We're happy as we are."

He felt Ed's gaze on him and deliberately didn't look in his direction. Uncomfortable with the deception in a way he'd never been before, he wasn't sure he could carry it off if he caught Ed's eye.

"So, James. What are you up to this weekend?" Ed asked, diverting the attention of the table away from Alec.

Alec glanced up, wondering whether it was deliberate. Either way, he was grateful the subject of Belinda had been dropped.

Dinner with the partners was the usual tedious mixture of shop talk, social chit-chat, and subtle brown-nosing. Alec was so expert at it after years of practice, that he was able to keep up his end of the conversation even while his mind was wandering.

He'd stayed up late the night before, trying to focus on work, but his thoughts had kept straying to Ed, and they were doing the same this evening while he was supposed to be impressing the partners. Luckily, Henry, one of the senior partners, was deep in a golfing anecdote that only required Alec to nod and chuckle at appropriate moments, so he seemed to be getting away with his daydreaming.

Alec had never been distracted like this before. He was used to being utterly single-minded, able to focus his razor-sharp mind exactly where he chose. But his wayward brain was full of thoughts of Ed.

This was why it was never a good idea to be involved with someone you worked with. Even if Alec wasn't in the closet, he couldn't have a relationship with Ed, not while Ed was on his team. It wasn't against company policy as such, but it was certainly frowned upon. Then again, Ed was only a temp. In a few weeks, he might be gone from Baker Wells completely or would at least have moved on to work elsewhere in the firm. And then....

And then you'll be free of distractions and able to get back to business as usual, he told himself firmly. Nothing else was an option.

He shook himself free of stupid fantasies and dragged his attention back to Henry, who was waiting for him to reply.

"Absolutely. I'm sure I can fit in a round of golf sometime. It's been a while, though. I fear my swing may need as much polishing as my clubs."

Henry chuckled. "It will all come back to you, like riding a bicycle. I'll have my PA call yours when the weather gets a little warmer, and we can set something up."

Alec noticed Belinda watching him, her clever eyes narrow and thoughtful. He'd never been able to hide anything from her. That was why she was the only person to know about his sexuality. He had a feeling she was going to get this new secret out of him too.

Sure enough, she rounded on him as soon as they got into the taxi after dinner. "Are you going to tell me what's up with you? Or am I going to have to drag it out of you?"

Alec could feel her expectant gaze on him. He avoided looking at her, focusing on the street outside instead as their cab pulled into the traffic. It was busy in Covent Garden tonight.

"It's nothing. Just work stress."

"Don't give me that bullshit, Alec Rowland. I've seen work stress on you before—it's a constant state—and this is not it. You've been distracted all evening. Now spill."

There was a long pause. Alec bit his lip and frowned, reluctant to put his dilemma into words.

"Alec?" Concern crept into Belinda's voice and she put a perfectly manicured hand on his knee. "You're worrying me now. Are you ill or something?"

"God, no. Stop being such a drama queen. It's nothing like that. I just…." He turned to her and lowered his voice. "I met someone a couple of weeks ago, and by 'met' I mean fucked. And then he showed up at work. He's the new guy on my team."

Her eyes flew wide and her mouth softened into a gentle "oh" of understanding. Because if anyone knew how closely he'd guarded his secret and how deep his fear of discovery was, it was Belinda.

"Does anyone else know?" she asked.

"No."

"Is he out?"

"Yes. Out and proud. He makes it look so fucking easy." Bitterness flooded Alec's words.

She squeezed his knee in sympathy. "I can see it must be freaking you out having to work with him. But surely he just wants to do his job. Can't you both pretend it never happened?"

Alec let out a bitter chuckle. "If only."

She frowned, the cogs turning, and Alec saw the inevitable realisation dawn.

"Oh my *God*. After all these years, someone's finally got to you? Fucking hell. I didn't think it was possible. Mr No Strings Attached is finally hooked."

He didn't bother to try denying it. What was the point? "If you could sound less gleeful about it, that would help." He glared at her. "This isn't something to be excited about. It's a fucking disaster."

The taxi was pulling up outside Belinda's flat now.

"Okay, yes, sorry. I didn't mean to be callous. I'm just in shock." She took his hand. "You're coming in for a drink. This conversation isn't over."

Alec was a lawyer. He knew when negotiation was possible and when it was a waste of oxygen. Anyway, a drink sounded like a great idea.

Inside her flat, Belinda switched on the lamps and kicked off her heels.

"Sit," she said, walking to the drinks cabinet to fetch glasses and a bottle.

Alec sat. Belinda's sofa was an enormous thing covered in red suede, with black-and-white polka-dot cushions.

"Whisky okay for you, darling?"

"Yes, thanks." Alec was already anticipating the comforting burn in his throat and the fire in his belly.

"So, tell me about him." She curled up at the opposite end of the sofa, facing him. "I want to know everything."

Alec took a deep breath and launched into an account of their meeting. He edited out some of the sexual highlights—not that Belinda would have minded the details, but Alec wanted to keep those for himself. Then he went on to describe Ed's position at Baker Wells and the interactions they'd had since he started to work there. When he got to the part about propositioning Ed last Friday, she gasped in horror.

"Oh, Alec. What on earth were you thinking by even suggesting it? It's so unlike you to be that rash."

"I wasn't thinking," he replied dryly. "Or at least, not with my brain."

She leaned forward to refill his glass with a generous slosh of the amber liquid. "This guy's really got to you, hasn't he?"

Alec took another long swallow as he thought about how to answer. His face heated, and he finally allowed himself to admit it out loud. "Yes, damn it. I can't stop thinking about him." He turned to meet her sympathetic gaze. "He's smart and funny, and there's a sweetness to him. It's impossible not to like him. This would be so much easier if it was only about sexual attraction. But it's more."

"So why don't you tell him that? He probably thinks you just want a convenient fuck. Maybe he'd feel differently if he knew this meant something to you."

"No. I have way too much to lose. I can't make myself any more vulnerable than I already have." It wasn't in Alec's nature to show his hand, professionally or personally. Knowledge was power, and although he might be drawn to Ed, he didn't know if he could trust him.

"What are you going to do, then?"

"Back to plan A, I suppose. Pretend that nothing ever happened, act like the professional I'm supposed to be, and hope I get over this ridiculous obsession soon." Alec turned the glass in his hand. He'd emptied it again already and the whisky in his veins was stirring him up, dragging his emotions too close to the surface. "Sometimes I wish I could find the courage to be honest about who I am." His voice betrayed him, going tight and hoarse as he fought back the loneliness that threatened to swamp him with miserable self-pity.

"Oh, darling." Belinda put her glass down and scooted along the sofa so she could put her arm around Alec and pull his head down to her shoulder.

"Life would be so easy if I was really in love with you," he murmured.

She chuckled. "Apart from the little detail that I'm not in love with *you*. Never have been, never will be. I adore you, but you're not my type."

Alec laughed. "Good point."

Belinda's type was rather more feminine than Alec. She had a penchant for androgynous-looking men—preferably blonds.

They slipped into a relaxed silence, and Alec let her hold him, enjoying the sensations of a warm body against his and gentle fingers combing through his hair. He realised how starved he was of touch as comfort poured into him, temporarily filling and soothing the empty space inside.

Plan A went fairly well for a few days. Alec continued to push Ed hard in the office, demanding 110 percent in everything he did. Much to Alec's frustration, Ed rose to every challenge and accepted each Herculean task with grace. It drove Alec crazy, because Alec wanted Ed to lose his cool. He wanted to see his temper flare, to have Ed push back and rebel. Alec wanted an excuse to yell at him, to relieve some of the unbearable tension between them.

Finally, on the Thursday night of Ed's third week, Alec had his chance.

They were the only two left there that night, working in one of the breakout rooms that led off their main office space. It was nearly ten, and even the cleaners had been and gone.

Alec had insisted Ed stay and go through the draft purchase agreement to check for errors. The agreement had been drafted by Alec, checked by James, and already approved by Katherine before coming back to Alec for a final read-through. Alec had said he wanted one more person to look it over before it went out to the clients. Ed had agreed, but when Alec refused to let him finish the work at home, Ed had done a poor job of hiding his irritation. He was currently hunched over his laptop with his back to Alec and his chin resting on his hand as he scrolled through the document.

"Okay, I'm done." He spun around on his chair, stretching his arms up and arching his spine. "It looks perfect. I didn't find anything that needs changing. Can I go home now?"

"Are you sure?" Alec asked.

"Yes. I'm sure." Ed's tone was carefully controlled, but there was a flare of challenge in his blue eyes that made Alec's heart beat faster.

"That's odd. Because when I went through it earlier, I noticed that all the references to the Vendor and the Purchaser in clause six are the wrong way around."

"What?" Ed turned back to his screen and started scrolling again. He rubbed his eyes and glared at the screen. "No way. Where?"

Alec got up and moved to stand by Ed's shoulder. He pointed at the offending word. "There."

Ed pushed his chair back and stood. His face was red and he clenched his fists. "You knew about that error all the time and you left it in there. For what? To test me?"

"This is your job, Ed. Don't be a baby about it," Alec said dismissively. He held Ed's furious gaze, a thrill of excitement and anticipation rippling through him as he waited for Ed to lose it. He could practically hear the time bomb ticking as Ed got closer to detonation. "Yes, it *was* a test, and you failed."

"I missed one detail, an error you knew was there all along. I've been here for nearly fifteen hours today, Alec. I can hardly see straight!"

Alec shrugged. "Even one tiny error in the paperwork reflects badly on our firm. It makes us look unprofessional."

Ed took a step closer. Right up in Alec's face now, he yelled. "You're a fine one to talk about being *professional*." He spat the word out. "For two weeks now, you've been on my back, giving me the shittiest of shitty jobs, and I've put up with it because I know that's how it's supposed to be. I'm the newest on the team. I need to prove I can hack it. But this *isn't* professional is it, Alec? It's personal. You're punishing me for fucking you, and it's not bloody *fair*. Because I didn't know, okay? When I let you pick me up in that bar, I didn't know you were going to be my new boss. And believe me, if I'd known what a controlling arsehole you are, I'd have run a mile before I'd have let your cock anywhere near me!"

He finally stopped for breath, panting and flushed.

They stared at each other. Stags locking horns. Alec's heart pounded as though he'd been running, and a heady cocktail of hormones and adrenaline coursed through his system. He brought his hand up and grabbed the front of Ed's shirt, balling it in his fist, pulling him closer. Ed's pupils dilated, but he didn't flinch away.

Alec kissed him.

Ed's mouth was open and slack with surprise, and as Alec tried to force his tongue inside, Ed twisted away so that Alec kissed his neck instead. He tasted the sweat of Ed's anger and felt the beat of the pulse in his throat. There was a vibration and he realised Ed was chuckling.

"Jesus Christ," Ed said in a hoarse voice. "Please tell me this isn't happening."

But then suddenly Ed was grabbing Alec and pulling him closer, and they were kissing in a furious clash of teeth and tongues as they stumbled back towards the nearest hard surface—which happened to be the edge of a desk. Ed's arse hit the wood, and Alec lifted him, pushing between Ed's thighs so their cocks aligned. He ground against Ed's hardness and Ed groaned. Ed untucked Alec's shirt at the waist and slid his hands under the fabric, digging his fingers so hard into Alec's skin he'd leave marks.

Alec found Ed's neck again and bit down, retaliating.

"Don't leave a mark where people can see this time, you fucker," Ed hissed.

Alec pushed up the front of Ed's shirt and bit his chest instead. He sucked on a nipple and then on the sensitive skin beside it, drawing a mark to the surface that would last for days. Then he moved to attack Ed's mouth again, kissing him deep and dirty, his hands in Ed's hair holding him in place as their hips moved together in a rhythm born of desperation.

Alec realised Ed had worked a hand between them and pushed it down the front of his trousers, jerking himself off. Ed didn't have much room to manoeuvre, but from the sounds he was making, it was obviously working. Alec was close too. He could probably come like this, with his tongue in Ed's mouth, grinding against the back of his hand, but he wanted more.

Before he could think better of it, he slid to his knees on the plush office carpet and started to open Ed's fly. He couldn't remember the last time he'd got down on his knees for someone, and it sent a long-forgotten shiver of delight through him. There was a freedom in giving pleasure like this, in allowing someone else to have him this way. Ed looked down, his eyes wide and pupils huge as Alec freed his erection from his trousers and underwear.

When Alec took Ed into his mouth, he imagined how this would look to someone walking into the office right now. Alec Rowland, Senior Associate, on his knees sucking the temp's cock. The thought of the spectacle they must make only turned him on more as the fear of discovery rippled through him. The risk was tiny. The only person in the building would be the night security guard, and he rarely left his desk. But there was a risk, nevertheless, and it only heightened Alec's arousal. He sucked Ed hard and fast. Now was not the time for slow and leisurely.

It seemed to be working for Ed. He slid his hands into Alec's hair. "Oh my God," he moaned.

CHAPTER SIX

Ed hadn't believed Alec when he said the work would get harder. He thought he'd already reached the limit of what the team could handle, but as the date for the final negotiations grew closer, the pressure increased.

Nearly two weeks had passed since the crazy night when Alec had blown him in the office and then stayed on his knees afterwards, hiding his face while Ed stroked his hair. Every time Ed looked at Alec, he remembered it vividly and was assaulted by a blend of tenderness and desire. But he was strung out on caffeine and adrenaline, and his brain was so stuffed full of facts, figures, and contract details that he didn't have much space left to try and sort through his feelings about Alec.

They hadn't been alone together since that night—whether by accident or design, Ed wasn't sure. He thought maybe Alec was avoiding him, and reluctantly accepted it was probably for the best.

The atmosphere between them had been easier, at least. The sex had softened something, smoothed away the spiky edges of their antagonism. Alec had been more courteous, more prone to smiling during their interactions. He was also more likeable than before, which only made it harder for Ed to accept that nothing could ever happen between them. Even though he knew it was stupid and it could never work out, Ed couldn't help entertaining

"You did well this week, Ed." Alec patted Ed's shoulder, needing to touch him one more time. "Catch up on some sleep this weekend, because the next few weeks are only going to get harder."

"Disturbingly?" Ed glanced up from fastening his fly.

"Being down on my knees isn't my usual MO, especially not on the office carpet."

Ed's lips twitched again as he hesitated for a moment, and then he grinned outright and said in a bold rush, "You look good on your knees."

Alec felt a confusing rush of arousal and irritation. That seemed to be his permanent state around Ed. "Yes, well. It can't happen again."

The smile left Ed's face abruptly. "No, of course not."

There were so many things Alec wanted to say: *I care about you. I want you, but I'm not as brave as you*. Instead he fell back on the easy explanation. "We need to keep this professional from now on."

"Fine by me," Ed said, but there was an edge to his voice that told Alec he wasn't the only one with mixed feelings.

Ed turned away and started to pack up his stuff. There wasn't anything left to say, so Alec did the same.

They waited for the lift together in silence.

The doors slid closed, trapping them in the small space, and Alec's gaze strayed to study Ed's reflection in the mirrored wall. He turned to Ed and lifted a hand to smooth his hair back into place where it was still ruffled from his hands earlier.

"Thanks." A ghost of a smile lit up the tired shadows on Ed's face.

The hint of stubble on Ed's cheek glinted golden in the light. Alec resisted the urge to brush a kiss over it. "You look knackered," he said.

Ed raised an eyebrow. "I wonder who's to blame for that?"

A jolt of electric need arrowed down to Alec's groin. He shoved his hand down his own waistband so he could grip his cock while he sucked, humping into his fist as he spiralled into mindless pleasure, his control slipping.

Ed's gaze caught the movement of Alec's arm. "Oh fuck, you're—God, Alec. You look so…."

He never finished the sentence, because he started to come. The pulse of Ed's dick and the taste of his release tipped Alec over and he shot into his hand and his underwear in a hot, sticky mess as he moaned around Ed's cock. Shame and satisfaction mingled, making him feel oddly vulnerable as he finally pulled off and pressed his face into Ed's hip while he caught his breath. He couldn't meet Ed's eyes, but he breathed in his scent as his heart rate settled and his breathing slowed. Ed's hands were still in Alec's hair, stroking lightly in an echo of Belinda's hands the week before, a touch offering comfort and affection. Alec's heart ached with wanting more of it. Was this what happened when you finally realised what you were missing out on?

"Alec?" Ed's voice was soft, and when Alec lifted his head to meet his gaze, Ed smiled uncertainly and stroked Alec's cheek. "Did you… um, want me to return the favour?"

"Too late." Alec pulled his wet hand out of his trousers and held it up. A thick web of come stretched between his thumb and forefinger.

Ed's lips quirked in amusement. "Oh, yeah. I wondered. I wasn't sure."

Alec flushed. "It's been a while." He got to his feet and pulled a handkerchief out of his pocket to wipe his hand. "And that was disturbingly hot."

occasional wild fantasies where Alec wanted him for more than a one-night stand or risky office sex.

Something in Alec called out to Ed. He was so aloof, so utterly in control of every situation in the workplace. But Ed had seen beneath that surface. He'd glimpsed the complexity of the man beneath the facade, and the loneliness and vulnerability he'd seen there made him want to smash a hole in those walls so that he could climb inside and pull Alec out. It hurt to think he'd never get the chance.

When he arrived at the office on Wednesday morning, Katherine was there, talking with Alec. Ed went to his desk and powered up his laptop, but the sound of his name drew his attention to their conversation.

"Take Ed with you," she was saying. "It'll be good experience for him to sit in on the meeting."

"I'm not sure there's any need," Alec replied. "We've already concluded most of the negotiations via conference call as you know. The meeting in Edinburgh is really a formality because Mackenzie wants to meet Maxwell in person. I think Ed's time would be better spent here, helping James with the last bits of paperwork."

Ed swivelled around on his office chair to look at them, wondering whether he was going to get any say in this discussion. Apparently not.

"Take him." Katherine's tone implied it wasn't worth arguing about. "I'll have Jen book rooms for both of you. The meeting's scheduled for Friday morning, so you fly up tomorrow evening. It could take all day to iron out the details, so I'll have her book two nights, and you'll travel back on

Saturday. Have you ever been to Edinburgh, Ed?" Katherine finally included him in the conversation.

"No."

"Well, it's a beautiful city. Make sure you take some time to enjoy it while you're there." She managed to make that sound like an order too. "Alec can show you the sights, I'm sure."

Ed nodded. "All right. That sounds fun."

Ed chanced a glance at Alec, who had his poker face firmly in place. Ed hoped his own expression wasn't giving away his inner thoughts right now, because *fuck*. Two nights in a hotel with Alec away from the workplace sounded like a dangerous, yet utterly thrilling prospect. For all their talk about keeping things professional, Ed was definitely going to pack some lube and condoms, just in case.

After work on Thursday, they got a taxi all the way from the office to Heathrow. Ed was horrified by the expense. He watched the price on the meter tick up and up and up, and he shook his head.

"We could have just got on a train and given this money to charity or something."

"I already give plenty of money to charity," Alec said. "And this way is much more comfortable, even if it takes ages — especially in the rush hour."

He had a point. Although secretly Ed wouldn't have minded being squashed up next to Alec in a crowded train carriage.

"You give money to charity?"

"Of course. I earn far more than I need. I invest some of it, and I also support causes I believe in."

"Which charity do you support?" Ed knew it was a nosy question, but he was intrigued.

"A charity that supports homeless LGBT youth." Alec avoided Ed's gaze, picking at the edge of one of his fingernails. "They do a lot of good work for young people who've been kicked out by their families or who've run away because they're afraid of what their families would do to them if they found out."

Something about Alec's tone set off alarm bells for Ed. "Did your parents find out about you?"

Alec's jaw tightened. He picked at his nail again and then cursed as he drew blood by pulling on a piece of loose skin.

"Alec?" Ed pressed.

"I was caught in a compromising position at school." Alec's voice was quiet and he spoke quickly, as though it was easier to say the words if he got them out fast. "I was expelled. My father wasn't too chuffed about that, as you can imagine. He used his belt on me the day I came home… called me a disgusting little queer."

Ed's mind flashed back to their first and only night together, and he had a sudden vivid memory of the faint scars he'd seen on Alec's back the next morning. He felt sick. He wanted to reach for Alec's hand and hold it, to stop Alec from hurting himself where he was worrying at the cut on his finger, but he was afraid Alec would push him away. "I'm sorry," he said instead. "I'm so sorry."

"Why? You weren't the one sucking my dick in the shrubbery." Alec's dry chuckle had no humour in it.

Ed couldn't bring himself to join in with Alec's attempt at a joke. Instead he said, "And now they believe you're straight?"

"I did a good job of convincing them I prefer girls. They were more than happy to believe me and write off my indiscretion as hormone-driven stupidity. That made me less of a disappointment."

Ed didn't know what to say. His mother had hugged him when he'd told her he was gay. She had told him she loved him and that all she wanted was for him to be happy. His heart hurt for Alec and the shame and hatred he still carried inside.

Alec carried on talking, filling the uncomfortable silence. "Of course, since I turned thirty a couple of years ago, they've ramped up the pressure on me to marry. They don't approve of Belinda, but they're desperate for grandchildren to carry on the Rowland name. My younger brother, Caspar, isn't showing any signs of settling down either — and any child he fathers is likely to be illegitimate. So I'm their best hope." Alec laughed bitterly. "Poor sods. One wayward son and one secretly gay one." He glanced at Ed, then looked out of the window. "Sorry. I'm banging on. I don't normally talk about this family stuff with anyone apart from Belinda." He looked embarrassed.

"It's okay," Ed said. And it was. He was flattered that Alec trusted him enough to open up and say the things he'd said. "Does Caspar know you're gay?"

"He may suspect," Alec replied. "He knows what happened at school, and I'm not sure he ever believed Belinda's really my girlfriend. But we haven't discussed it for years."

"Would he care?"

"I doubt it. He works in the fashion industry. He has plenty of gay friends, so I can't imagine he'd have a problem with it."

"Maybe you should tell him."

"Maybe." Alec changed the subject. "What's your family like?"

"Very different to yours, by the sound of it. My mum and stepdad are pretty great. We clashed sometimes when I was a teenager, like everyone does, but they were awesome when I came out."

"Have you got brothers and sisters?"

"Three sisters. Well… half-sisters." Ed smiled as he thought of the girls. "They're monkeys, especially the twins." He launched into some anecdotes to make Alec smile, and by the time they got to the airport, the atmosphere had lifted.

On the plane, Alec took the seat by the window.

"This is so exciting," Ed said, leaning across him to peer out of the window as the plane moved along the runway. "I haven't been on a plane in ages, not since I went to Ibiza the summer after I did my A levels." He blushed. "Sorry, I sound like such a hick. I expect you fly all the time, don't you?"

"Quite a bit, yes."

Something about Alec's tone made Ed look at him more closely. Alec was rigid with tension. He was breathing slowly and deeply, but his face was pale and there was a tightness to his expression.

"Are you okay?" Ed asked cautiously. Alec had the look of a man who might bite his head off for asking.

The note of the engines changed as the plane sped up, and a muscle ticked in Alec's jaw. "I'm not a fan of flying. But I'll be a little better once we're in the air."

"Oh, right. Not long now."

The engines roared; the final thrust of acceleration pushed Ed back into the seat, and his stomach swooped as the plane lifted off the runway into the evening sky.

Ed couldn't resist leaning across Alec again to watch as the lights of the city fell away beneath them and the plane banked, curving around to head north. Exhilarated, Ed grinned at Alec, who still looked as though he were carved out of granite. "They'll bring the drinks trolley round soon. You look like you need one."

Alec glanced sidelong at him, and his lips twisted into a tight smile. "Yes. Apparently alcohol helps enormously in the event of a plane crash."

Ed chuckled.

Even when the seat belt lights went off, Alec was still tense, so Ed distracted him by pulling out the draft purchase agreement and notes for the meeting tomorrow. He knew Alec would be able to focus on those, and maybe it would stop him being afraid that the plane was about to fall out of the sky.

Sure enough, Ed's questions and queries soon had Alec focused on him rather than their surroundings. Ed hid a smile, relaxing as Alec's tension eased.

When the cabin crew came around offering drinks, Alec asked for mineral water and Ed followed his lead. He was tired, and alcohol would only make him sleepy. He wanted to be able to focus on what Alec was saying. Tomorrow was a big day.

They landed unscathed, and Alec's relief as the wheels touched down smoothly on Scottish soil was apparent. The colour came back to his cheeks, and he smiled sheepishly at Ed. "Thanks for not taking the piss. Whenever I fly with James, he's a total arse about it."

"You should see me if I'm faced with a spider," Ed grinned. "I'm in no position to judge anyone with an irrational fear of anything. Plus hardly any spider in this country is an actual threat, whereas people *do* die in plane crashes. So your phobia is way more logical than mine."

"You're really scared of spiders?"

"Terrified. I literally scream like a teenage girl. Fiona, my housemate, has to save me from the giant ones in the bathtub on a regular basis."

Alec laughed. "Thanks. I feel better now."

"You're welcome."

By the time they got to their hotel, it was nearly nine in the evening.

"I'm starving," Alec said in the lift up to their floor. "It's a bit late for the restaurant. How about you get settled, then come to my room to go through the final details for tomorrow, and we can order room service?"

"Okay." Ed tried not to flush at the thought of being alone in a hotel room with Alec. *You're a professional*, he reminded himself. *He's your boss. You're not going there again*.

After he'd unpacked his case, Ed walked along the corridor to Alec's room a few doors down. He knocked, and was greeted with "Come in, it's open."

Alec was sprawled on his bed already surrounded by papers. He was still in his shirt and suit trousers, but his feet were bare, and he had draped his tie over the back of a chair along with his suit jacket. The sleeves of his shirt were rolled up and dark chest hair showed at the open neck.

Ed swallowed hard, desperately trying to tamp down his libido, because Jesus Christ, Alec wasn't making this whole professional-relationship thing easy looking like that. Ed had been tempted to change into jeans and a T-shirt but had deliberately kept on his suit jacket and tie, needing that formality to remind him of their roles. He walked to the window, allowing the impressive view outside to distract him from the sight of Alec.

"Wow, is that Edinburgh Castle?" He stared at the floodlit building, high up on its rocky crag in the centre of the city. "It's amazing."

"It's beautiful, isn't it?"

Ed stopped to admire it a moment longer, before turning back to Alec.

"I thought it was easier to spread this lot out on the bed," Alec said. "But it won't take long to go through it. We covered most of it on the flight. I'm just putting it all in order for tomorrow."

Ed toed off his shoes and took a seat beside Alec, leaning back against the headboard and crossing his legs at the ankle.

"Oh, and here's the room service menu." Alec passed it to him. "Work out what you want, and then can you order? I'll have the Aberdeen Angus steak sandwich with salad rather than chips."

They tidied the papers away before their food came. All neatly filed and organised, ready for the meeting tomorrow morning.

"You won't need to do anything other than observe," Alec reassured him as he put everything back in his briefcase. "I'm not anticipating any major quibbles. I think Mr Mackenzie prefers doing business face-to-face. He's old-school, and he's been running this chain for thirty years. He wants to see who he's selling to, to be sure it's going to a good home."

"And what if our client fails to reassure him?" Ed asked.

"He won't. Maxwell runs a tight ship, but his reputation in the industry is impeccable and he's very good at charming people."

A knock on the door distracted them. A young woman, about Ed's age, wheeled in a trolley with their meals. Ed watched as Alec thanked her, giving her a generous tip.

"Thank you, sir." She smiled and flushed. "Can I help you with anything else?"

"No thanks. Good night." Alec turned to the trolley, passing Ed the plate with a gourmet burger on it and picking up his own steak sandwich.

Ed noticed with amusement that the woman stole a final glance at Alec over her shoulder as she let herself out. He couldn't blame her. Alec was worth a second look.

"Poor girl nearly tripped over her tongue," he commented as Alec sat back down.

"What?"

"Staring at you like you were on the menu."

"Oh." Alec's lips quirked. "Well, she's out of luck."

Aren't we all, thought Ed rather morosely.

They ate in silence sitting side by side on the bed with their legs stretched out. Ed looked at Alec's bare feet next to his socked ones. It felt oddly intimate, and maybe that was what gave him the courage to ask something he'd been wondering about for a while.

"So, that first time we met... is that what you usually do for sex? Pick up randoms in clubs?"

"It works for me." Alec's tone was frosty.

"Sorry, I didn't mean to sound judgemental. I mean, I was there—right? I was up for it too."

"So I recall." The ice melted again and humour crept in.

Ed glanced sideways and flushed when their gazes met. "Yeah. Um. So you've never, like, dated or anything? Nothing more permanent?"

"You're a lawyer, Ed. Try and sound the part. No hesitation, no deviation. Just ask what you want to know."

"Have you ever had a boyfriend?"

Alec shook his head. "No. But I've never wanted one. There are fewer and fewer men who are prepared to stay in the closet these days. Boyfriends tend to want to do inconvenient stuff like be seen in public together. It's easier to pick someone up when I want a warm body to fuck instead of my hand." He folded his arms defensively.

His words stung. "Don't you get lonely?" Ed pressed.

"I don't have time to be lonely."

"I don't believe you."

"Believe what you like. Anyway, I assume you're not seeing anyone? Nothing serious if you were prepared to go home with me. So, aren't you lonely too?"

"Sometimes," Ed replied honestly. "I don't live alone, though. I have a housemate. But I miss being in a relationship. I had a long-term boyfriend while I was at university, but it didn't work out." Ed's gut twisted with the remembered pain of that relationship breakdown. "There hasn't been anyone serious since. I hope I'll find that closeness again sometime."

"I'm sure you will." Alec balled his napkin and stacked their empty plates. He got up and carried them over to the desk. With his back to Ed, he checked his watch and said, "We should hit the hay. We need to be in Mackenzie's office for nine thirty."

The time for confidences was clearly over. Disappointment nagged at the edges of Ed's consciousness as he sat on the edge of the bed and put his shoes back on. He sighed, telling himself he was stupid for hoping for anything to happen. It was better this way. Less complicated. But he couldn't tamp down the feeling of wistfulness, of a chance missed. Maybe in some parallel universe there was an Ed who'd managed to break past Alec's reserve, but in this one, Alec's walls had come back up. "Goodnight, Alec."

Alec glanced up from checking his phone. "Night, Ed. Sleep well."

Back in his room, Ed took off his trousers and hung them up, then unbuttoned his shirt before heading into the bathroom for a piss. When he'd finished, he went to the sink to brush his teeth and jumped out of his skin with a yelp. "Oh Jesus, *fuck*!"

He stared in horror, his heart pounding.

An enormous spider stared back. It looked as if it was staring, anyway, with all eight of its evil little eyes.

Ed hadn't been kidding when he told Alec about his phobia. The idea of spending the night anywhere near this monster was intolerable. He picked up a glass and tiptoed closer. Maybe if he could trap it, he could put it out of the window or something. He knew it was stupid, but he didn't like killing them. It wasn't their fault he loathed the bloody things.

Ed paused, ready to pounce. He was sure it was watching him. He moved the glass closer, slowly edging it over the spider. God, it was so huge he wasn't sure he could catch it under the glass without squashing its hairy legs.

Ed lowered the glass, slowly, imperceptibly, trying to keep his breathing calm and even and to not freak out. He was almost there. Just another couple of inches and he'd have it….

But then the spider moved, rushing towards Ed with intent. Ed yelled and smashed the glass down, trying to catch it. The glass shattered against the porcelain of the sink and exploded, sending shards everywhere. In a panic, Ed stumbled back and then howled with pain as he stood on a shard of glass, driving it into his foot.

"Fucking bastard spider!" he yelled. "You evil fucker!"

Ed retreated to the bedroom, slamming the bathroom door shut, and sat on the bed to check out the damage. He winced when he saw the piece of glass still sticking out of his foot. It wasn't huge, but it hurt and his foot was oozing blood. Gritting his teeth, he pulled it out carefully, then wadded up a tissue and pressed it against the cut to try to stop the bleeding.

God, he still needed to brush his teeth and get ready for bed, and fucking glass was everywhere — plus the spider was still in his bathroom. Ed's phone was sitting on the table by the bed. Before he had time to think better of it, he texted Alec.

SOS. Spider attack. Help me!

It was only after Ed pressed Send that he realised he could have called the front desk and got them to send someone up to sort out the mess and deal with the spider while they were at it.

But Alec replied immediately. *Are you serious?*

Deadly. It's trying to kill me. Please come.

He hoped Alec would see the funny side.

When he heard the knock on the door, Ed hobbled to open it.

"What the hell's going on in here?" Alec looked Ed up and down. Ed had forgotten he was only wearing boxers and a shirt that was open at the front until Alec's gaze raked over him. Alec was still fully dressed, with his shoes now back on.

"There's a spider." Ed gestured towards the bathroom with the bloody tissue he was still clutching in his hand. "I tried to catch it, but I broke a glass, and then I cut my foot."

"You're a disaster."

Ed didn't try to deny it. Instead he limped pitifully back to his bed and sat on the edge with his foot pulled up into his lap. "At least it's not a pale carpet."

Alec knelt down. His hands were gentle as he probed the bloody sole of Ed's foot and located the cut on his heel. "It's not too bad. Feet bleed a lot, especially if you're running around. Lie down and elevate it. Keep pressure on it too. I've got a first aid kit in my case. I'll go and get it. I assume you don't have one?"

Ed shook his head. "I'm not that organised."

He followed Alec's instructions, lying down and propping his foot up on his opposite knee. He clamped the wad of tissues Alec had left him with over the cut, and cursed the universe, all spiders, and his own clumsiness.

When Alec came back, he examined Ed's cut again. "It's just about stopped bleeding, but I think we need to give it a bit longer to clot before I dress it. You stay there. I'm going to check out the damage in the bathroom."

"Be careful," Ed said. "That spider is evil."

"I think I can handle it." Alec went into the bathroom. "Bloody hell." His voice echoed through to the bedroom. "What a mess. Where was the spider?"

"In the sink," Ed called. Then he added, "Please don't kill it."

"Seriously?" Alec sounded incredulous.

"I don't like killing them," Ed admitted in a small voice.

"Okay," Alec said, then, "*wow*. That is big." There was silence for a moment, and then Alec muttered, "Come on, you bugger." His voice rose a little. "No. Don't you dare go up my sleeve — Gotcha!"

Alec emerged triumphant, his hands clasped in front of him. "I've got it."

Ed shuddered. "Where are you going to put it?"

"Oh, yes. Good point. Can you open the window?"

Ed got up and tiptoed across the room, trying not to put his heel down on the carpet. He slid up the sash window, and then stood aside and watched, half-admiring, half-horrified, as Alec reached out onto the sill and opened his hands so that the spider could scuttle away. As soon as Alec's hands were back inside, Ed slammed the window shut.

"Thank you." He grinned at Alec. "My knight in shining armour."

"Go and lie back down before you start bleeding again."

Alec called the front desk and asked them to send someone to clean up the glass. Then he sat on Ed's bed and started rifling through his first aid kit. First he cleaned the cut carefully with antiseptic wipes that stung like a bitch. Ed bit his lip to stop himself from hissing, but he couldn't help flinching when Alec dabbed at it for a second time.

"Sorry," Alec glanced up at him, one hand holding Ed's foot firmly so that he couldn't jerk it away. "But you don't want to get an infection and have your foot drop off."

Ed snorted. "Did you ever consider an alternative career in medicine? Because your bedside manner is really quite special."

Alec laughed as he went back to cleaning the cut, and the sound made warmth spread in Ed's belly. He wanted to hear that more.

There was a knock at the door. Alec got up to let in the poor sod whose job it was to clean up after Ed.

"I'm so sorry," Ed heard him say. "My friend had a little run-in with a spider."

Ed cringed, glad he couldn't see around the corner in the L-shaped room to the bathroom door.

Alec returned and sat down again, pulling Ed's foot into his lap as the sound of a vacuum cleaner started up in the bathroom. "Let's get a plaster on you, so you can walk around your room without leaving a trail of gore behind you."

It crossed Ed's mind that he could easily be doing this himself. But Alec seemed to be enjoying playing doctor, and Ed wasn't complaining. Alec took his time selecting a dressing, and as he smoothed it onto Ed's foot, Ed flinched again.

"Sorry, did I hurt you?"

"No. It tickled."

Alec smiled. "Ah."

They stared at each other for a moment. Ed's foot still in Alec's lap, and Alec's hand resting lightly on Ed's ankle.

"I'm all finished" came a female voice with a strong Scottish accent from around the corner.

"Oh, cool. Hang on a sec," Ed called, trying to sit up so he could go and give the poor woman a tip for clearing up his mess.

But Alec beat him to it, already reaching into his pocket as he stood. "Thank you," Alec said smoothly. "Sorry to have troubled you so late."

"Och, its nae bother, sir. Thank you. Have a good evenin'."

The door clicked shut and they were alone again.

Alec came back into view, but he stopped at the foot of the bed, his hands in his pockets as his gaze raked over Ed where he lay sprawled on top of the covers.

"If I leave you to it, will you survive till morning?" he asked, lips curving. A dimple Ed had never noticed before pressed into his cheek.

Ed's heart skipped a little faster. "I don't know. It's a tough call. What if the spider has a family? Like a spider mafia. They might come looking for me."

"I think we'll have to take that chance." Alec approached the bed and started packing up his first aid kit.

Ed wanted to reach out, touch his hand and ask him to stay. But he didn't want to ruin this new atmosphere of levity between them by risking rejection, and they both needed sleep. They had a job to do tomorrow. "Thank you," he said quietly instead.

"You're welcome." Alec's smile was soft and made Ed's heart thump hopefully. "You can text me again if you get attacked by any more marauding spiders."

Ed chuckled. "Good to know I have backup. Thanks. Night, Alec."

"Night, Ed."

CHAPTER SEVEN

Alec woke early, feeling unusually refreshed. After he'd left Ed's room last night, he'd gone straight to bed and slept almost immediately. His head had been full of thoughts of Ed, but they hadn't kept him awake.

Wide awake with an hour to spare before breakfast, Alec went down to the hotel pool and swam laps until his shoulders burned. Back in his room, he considered going straight down to breakfast, but the urge for Ed's company had him picking up his phone. It was an urge that had become familiar over the last couple of weeks, and one he usually tried to resist.

Morning. Have you eaten yet? he sent.

No, came the reply.

Are you ready to go down for breakfast?

I can be in 5.

I'll call for you on my way past.

When Alec knocked on the door, Ed opened it quickly. His smile of greeting made Alec's heart beat harder.

"You survived the spider apocalypse, then?" Alec deadpanned. "Glad to see you made it through the night."

"Seems that way." Ed flushed a little, ducking his head so his golden brown fringe flopped into his eyes. He normally used some product to slick it back when he was at work, but this morning it looked as though he was fresh out of the shower and his hair was damp and soft. It made him look younger. "I'm sorry about last night. I feel like a bit of an idiot this morning."

"You are an idiot," Alec said.

Ed jerked his head up to meet Alec's gaze, but when he saw Alec was smiling, he grinned back. "Fuck off."

"That's no way to talk to your boss. Let's go. I'm starving."

Ed stepped into the corridor and pulled his door shut. He winced as he moved.

Alec frowned. "How's your foot this morning?"

"A bit sore. I won't be running any marathons today. But I'll get by."

Alec was relieved the meeting went as smoothly as he'd predicted. Their London client, Mr Maxwell, seemed to make a good impression on Mr Mackenzie.

There was a little quibbling over some of the covenants, but Alec had drafted them so tightly that it was easy for Maxwell to concede a couple and let Mackenzie feel he'd won a few points. Maxwell was good at that sort of thing, and when the meeting ended, he and Mackenzie were on good terms.

The whole thing took less time than they'd anticipated. Alec had expected the meeting to drag on into the afternoon, but they were finished by midday. Normally he would have tried to rearrange his flight and travel back to London that afternoon. Staying somewhere to sightsee was an unnecessary luxury he didn't usually permit himself, but the extra night was already booked and so were the flights for tomorrow. Alec wasn't going to turn down this unexpected chance to spend some time with Ed away from the office.

He knew it was dangerous. His feelings for Ed had only intensified in the two weeks since they'd had sex—crazy, risky sex that could have lost them their jobs if they'd been caught. The sensible thing to do this afternoon would be to go their separate ways and put some distance between them again for Alec's sanity. But Alec was tired of resisting. The pull towards Ed was too strong, and he wanted to test it out, to see whether Ed was as powerless to fight it as he was.

In the cab on the way back to their hotel, Alec turned to Ed.

"So"—he spread his hands—"we have the rest of the day free. What do you want to see?"

Ed's face lit up. "Really? Do we get to be tourists? I thought we'd have more work to do."

"It can wait till Monday—or at least until Sunday. Katherine's bound to quiz you about the trip when we get back to the office. She told you to sightsee remember? Katherine's not a woman you want to disobey."

Ed chuckled. "You're probably right. But I have no clue. The only thing I know about Edinburgh is there's a castle—which I've already seen from your window—and lots of hills. What do you suggest?"

"Well, I'm assuming you won't want to walk too far, so we might be best to avoid the hills. Shame, because Arthur's Seat is lovely and the views are great from the top." Ed had been trying to hide his limp, but Alec could tell his foot was hurting. "Although it's bloody cold, it's supposed to stay dry all day. So I thought maybe an open-top bus tour?"

"That sounds perfect."

After going back to their rooms to change, they met in the lobby. Alec got down there first, and when he saw Ed step out of the lift, his breath caught. The only other time he'd seen Ed in jeans was that first night in the club. These jeans were slightly less provocative. Slim legged but not superskinny, they showed off Ed's lean legs and hips. On top he wore a thick jumper and a Puffa jacket, and he was carrying a scarf and hat. He paused, looking around the lobby before catching sight of Alec.

Ed smiled as he approached. "I've never seen you in casual clothes before. I nearly didn't recognise you." His gaze skimmed down appreciatively over Alec, making Alec's skin prickle.

Alec was in jeans too, with a charcoal wool coat buttoned up tight in anticipation of the February chill. He already had his hat on, a grey knitted one pulled down over his ears. "Shall we?" He inclined his head towards the door.

"Lead on." Ed put on his hat and wrapped his scarf around his neck.

The tour buses stopped just a few hundred yards away from the hotel and ran every ten minutes or so. They were both hungry, so they bought sandwiches from a deli opposite and ate them at the bus stop while they waited.

When the bus came, Alec let Ed get on first and followed him up the steep steps to the top floor. He couldn't resist admiring Ed's arse as he climbed. The muscles flexed, the delicious curves right at Alec's eye level.

Ed went towards the front of the bus. It was busy, but there were a few spare seats. Ed slid into one a couple of rows back from the front. The seat behind him was free too. Alec hesitated for a moment, not sure whether to take the other double seat for himself. But Ed patted the seat beside him. "It's pretty full," he said as Alec joined him. "I'm sure they'll need the other seats soon."

Ed's breath clouded in the chilly air as he spoke. His smile was bright like the winter sunshine pouring from a sky the colour of his eyes. Dazzled by Ed as much as the sun, Alec sat, and the bus jolted into movement.

They stayed on board for most of the tour. The views from the top deck were good and it was a wonderful way to see the city. Alec had visited many times before, but the beautiful grey stone buildings never failed to be impressive.

Ed was fun to do this with because his enthusiasm was infectious. "It's such a beautiful city," he said, snapping yet another photo with his phone. "I wish we could walk more of it today, but my foot is grateful for the bus."

"If we come back another time, we should walk up Arthur's Seat," Alec said before he realised how that sounded. "I mean… if you get another chance to visit Edinburgh. It's a lovely walk. I recommend it."

Ed flashed him a quick look; his expression was hard to read. "Maybe one day."

By mutual agreement they got off the bus near the museum and wandered around in there for an hour or so. Strolling around slowly together, Alec couldn't shake the feeling that this was like a date. He kept stealing glances at Ed and wishing it really was. He wanted to touch him, to hold his hand. Alec had never wanted to hold another man's hand before. Ed made him want so many things he'd never imagined until recently.

Ed was charmed by the Lewis chessmen. "They're so cool. I've only ever seen photos of them before. I love their expressions. Such intensity, and the workmanship is incredible."

They got takeaway coffees at the museum café before heading back out into the streets.

"Are you okay to walk a little more?" Alec asked. Ed was still limping slightly, but he hadn't complained about it.

"Yeah. It's nice to see some of the city from street level."

"Okay, good. Because you can't come to Edinburgh without seeing the statue of Greyfriars Bobby. It's a must for all tourists."

"Greyfriars what?" Ed frowned.

As they walked, Alec told Ed the story of the devoted little dog who'd sat on his master's grave and refused to leave after leading the funeral procession. Ed was silent, listening intently. "He stayed there round the clock, only leaving once a day to eat," Alec said. "People tried to entice him away, but he refused, so eventually they built a shelter for him. Fourteen years he guarded his master's grave until he died himself."

"Oh my God." Ed's voice was choked. "That's so sad, but it's also one of the most adorable things I've ever heard. What loyalty!"

"I know." Alec swallowed down the lump in his own throat.

"Bollocks." Ed wiped his eyes and sniffed. "You made me cry."

"I'm sorry." Alec managed an apologetic grin.

"Freaking out over spiders, crying over heartbreaking tales of canine devotion. You're really seeing me at my best this weekend. This is not what I need when I'm trying to impress you."

"You are?" Hope leapt in Alec's chest.

"Of course." Ed looked at him as if he was stupid. "You're my boss."

"Oh, yes." Alec could have kicked himself. "Well, compassion isn't a bad quality in a lawyer, so I won't hold it against you. And we're even on the phobia front, so you don't lose any points there either."

"Glad to hear it."

They'd arrived at the statue of Greyfriars Bobby now. A small crowd of tourists gathered around it were touching its nose for luck and taking photos.

"Want me to take your picture?" Alec offered.

"Sure." Ed touched his forefinger to the little dog's nose, where it was polished gold by the touch of hundreds of thousands of tourists who'd gone before.

"Smile through your tears," Alec said as he lined up the shot.

"Very funny."

"Here you go." Alec showed his phone screen to Ed. He'd captured Ed smiling, a dimple softening his cheek. He tapped the screen a few times, sending the picture to Ed's phone. "I've texted it to you." He let his thumb hover over the photo for a second, deciding against deleting it. Sentimental, maybe, but he couldn't bring himself to wipe the image from his phone. He wanted to keep the memory of this afternoon.

They got back to the hotel around half past five after riding the open-top bus back through rush-hour traffic. It was almost dark now and the castle was lit up, spectacularly dominating the middle of the city.

Ed watched the sights, and Alec watched Ed.

Want and hope warred with doubt. If he made a move now, would Ed give him another chance? And if he did, what would they do when they were back in London next week? What did Alec even want from Ed? In the short term, he wanted whatever Ed would give him, but Alec was afraid it would never be enough.

"What do you want to do for dinner?" he finally asked, trying to keep his tone casual.

Ed turned to look at him and shrugged. "I'm easy." There was a glint in his eye and a quirk to his lips that made Alec take the challenge.

"Not always, if I recall correctly."

Ed laughed. "True. But about food, I am. I eat anything."

"Would you prefer to eat in the hotel, or go out?"

"Out. I'm greedy for more of the city, and it's a gorgeous evening." The sky was still clear, the deep blue of twilight fading to black.

"Okay. I know a nice Italian place that's not too far from the hotel. How does that sound?"

"Perfect."

In his room, Alec debated changing into something more formal for dinner. But he was comfortable in his jeans and henley, and the restaurant he was taking Ed to wasn't the sort of place they needed to be smart. He ran a comb through his short dark hair and brushed his teeth — pretty pointless given that he was probably about to go and eat something involving a ton of garlic, but he wanted to make the effort.

It's not a date, he reminded himself. *It's just two colleagues going out for a meal.*

But as he walked along the corridor to Ed's room, heart pounding and palms damp with sweat, it felt exactly like a date.

"Hi, I'm almost ready." Ed was wearing the same jeans as earlier but had traded his jumper for a blue-and-grey checked shirt over a white T-shirt. He pulled on a black pea coat and buttoned it up as Alec waited, and then wound his scarf around his neck. "I had a shower and my hair's still damp." He ran his hands through it. "I'm going to have terrible hat hair in the restaurant."

Alec smiled. "I promise not to laugh."

Ed's limp was a little worse as they walked along the street outside their hotel.

Alec slowed his pace to match Ed's. "Are you okay to walk? We can grab a taxi if you need?"

"No. I love cities at night. I'd rather see it from the street than through a taxi window."

They strolled slowly through the bustling streets where the shops were still open and lit up. Their route took them up a hill, away from the castle, and gradually the streets got quieter and narrower.

"We're nearly there," Alec said to Ed, who was clearly uncomfortable but trying to hide it.

"Is it that obvious?" he asked wryly. "It's really not too bad considering I've walked on it a lot today. You know how cuts hurt more when they start to heal? I feel it every time I put weight on it. But it'll be fine in a day or two."

The restaurant was small and cosy. Alec had eaten there once before, a couple of years ago when he was up in Edinburgh with Belinda for the Festival, and while he'd remembered the food was good, he'd forgotten the intimacy of the setting. Run by a Scottish-Italian family, it was all dim lights and candles, with sumptuous dark-red-and-gold decor. At least half of the other tables were already occupied and the rest of the diners were exclusively couples.

Their waiter, a beautiful young man with dark hair and eyes, led them to a table for two in a secluded corner. Alec's skin prickled as he felt the young man assessing and cataloguing them. He wondered what assumptions he might be making.

The waiter handed them menus and a wine list, and Ed smiled and thanked him. Alec nodded more curtly. His cheeks and neck were hot with a blush. He hoped it wasn't visible in the candlelight.

When the waiter had gone, Ed said, "This place is nice."

Alec met his gaze over the flickering candle. There was a single red rose in a vase on their table.

"It's a little more… romantic than I remembered," Alec admitted. "I think we're the only people in here who aren't on a date."

"Well, that's not too surprising."

Alec frowned. "Um, why?"

Ed grinned. "It's Valentine's Day on Sunday."

"Oh God, of course."

"I guess Belinda doesn't expect a card from you, then?"

Alec chuckled. "Not so much, no."

"I can't believe you didn't realise. And here I was thinking you were trying to woo me." Ed's voice was light and teasing, but the heat in his eyes made Alec's heart surge.

There was a long drawn-out pause while Alec wrestled with himself. Ed was flirting. He was there for the taking if Alec wanted, and God… Alec wanted him so much. Was it madness to go there again? Was it fair on either of them when it could only be another hookup? They could have another night together, but then what? It would only make things harder.

Ed smiled at him, a slow, dirty twist of his lips as he raised his eyebrows in unspoken challenge. *I'm here. I want you. What are you going to do about it?*

Ed might as well have spoken the words out loud because they were written all over his face.

Alec licked his lips and Ed's eyes tracked the movement. "Do you want me to woo you?" Alec managed. Not his smoothest line, but the best he could come up with over the thud of his pulse in his ears.

"I'm not averse to a bit of wooing. It would make a nice change from a quickie in the office."

They were putting their cards on the table, then. *Okay*, if Ed was brave enough to be honest, Alec could respond in kind. "It can only be tonight. Just one more night, Ed." Alec's chest hurt as he said the words. "I can't offer you more than that."

"I know. But I'll take it." Ed's face softened. "Just for tonight, can we imagine none of the other complicated shit exists? Pretend we're two normal guys on a Valentine's date and see what happens?"

Alec wanted that so much. "I've never been on a date before."

"Well, if it's your first time, I promise to be gentle. So, can we?"

Alec hesitated for a few seconds more, but then his desire for connection, for romance, for *Ed* won out over his fears. "Yes," he said softly. Relief and happiness flooded him as he dismantled the walls around himself to allow Ed in—at least temporarily. "Yes. Let's try it."

It turned out to be so much easier than he expected. They ordered food and a bottle of red, and Ed banned all work-related talk. So they talked more about their families and their childhoods.

Ed's background was so different to Alec's. His family lived hand-to-mouth rather than enjoying the money and privilege Alec had grown up taking for granted. Yet the way Ed spoke about his mum and stepdad made Alec ache for that easy acceptance, the unconditional love he'd never felt from his own parents.

Alec kept those thoughts to himself, not wanting to put a damper on the evening, but more than ever he realised how isolated he was. This weekend with Ed was like a shining, stolen moment of someone else's life: someone who let people in instead of shutting them out, someone who wasn't afraid to let himself care, to let himself fall in love.

Alec's reserve melted in the warmth of Ed's company, and when Ed pressed his ankle against

Alec's under the table, Alec ignored the instinct to pull away and kept his leg there.

Neither of them wanted dessert, but they ordered liqueur coffees. As Ed sipped at his, he fiddled with the teaspoon, spinning it on the dark red tablecloth as they talked. Alec realised Ed was as nervous as he was, and that gave him the courage to reach out and deliberately touch his hand. He put his hand over Ed's, stilling the movement of Ed's fidgeting and locking their fingers together.

Ed jerked his head up and met Alec's gaze. "What are we doing?"

"I don't know," Alec replied honestly. "I just know I have to do it."

Ed nodded. "Me too."

They stared at each other, fear and uncertainty reflecting back and forth.

"Shall we go?" Alec asked.

"Yes," Ed replied softly.

They didn't even wait for the bill. Alec left enough cash on the table to cover it along with a generous tip.

Out in the darkness of the street, Ed took Alec's hand. "Is this okay?"

"It's good." Alec squeezed Ed's hand, their bare fingers already cooling in the freezing night air. They should probably put gloves on, but he wanted to feel Ed's skin.

He forgot about Ed's sore foot until Ed tugged on his hand.

"Alec, can you slow down a little?"

"Sorry, Hopalong." Alec grinned. "I forgot." He let go of Ed's hand and wrapped an arm around him instead, encouraging Ed to lean on him. "Better?"

"Much." Ed put his arm around Alec's waist and held on tight.

When they turned down a side street where it was quieter and darker, Alec couldn't wait anymore. He brought them to a stop and tugged Ed around to face him.

"What?" Ed's face was beautiful, his features heightened by the play of light and shadow.

Alec put his hands up to touch Ed's cheeks, then slid his hands around the back of Ed's neck and pulled him gently into a kiss. Ed made a soft, humming sound of approval, wrapping his arms around Alec until their bodies were fused. His lips were cool, but the inside of his mouth was warm and sleek.

They kissed until Alec was breathless. He pulled away to stare at Ed again. Giddy with the wild, reckless freedom of kissing Ed like this, out under the sky instead of hidden away, he smiled wide and joyful, and Ed smiled back.

They kissed again in the hotel lift. Alec couldn't wait. Impatient and desperate, it was as though the years had dropped away and he was a teenager again. He'd kissed countless men before, he'd fucked and sucked, but he'd never felt like this. Everything was new and thrilling and terrifying all at once.

"My room?" he asked as the lift reached their floor. He was suddenly afraid Ed might pull away, that he might have changed his mind.

"Yours has the better view, but do you have condoms?"

"Fuck, no." Alec couldn't believe he hadn't thought of that. "I'll run back down and find a late-night shop or a pub with a machine in the toilets."

"I've got some. Let's go to my room." Ed took Alec's hand and tugged him along the corridor.

"You packed some?" Alec wasn't sure whether to be flattered or offended that Ed thought he was so easy.

"I didn't think I'd get to use them, but now I'm glad for my relentless optimism. It paid off for once."

As soon as they were inside Ed's room with the door locked behind them, they kissed again. Desperate for Ed's skin, for his touch, Alec didn't know where to begin. He didn't want to stop kissing him, but he wanted him naked. They stripped each other between kisses, cursing as buttons stuck and heads got trapped in T-shirts, but somehow they managed to get all their clothes off.

"Hang on. Lube and condoms are in the bathroom." Ed went to get them.

Alec watched his arse as he went, and admired the sway of his hard cock as he returned.

"Here." Ed tossed the supplies down on the bed.

They paused then, facing each other.

"What do you want to do?" Ed asked.

"Anything. Everything. Whatever you want?"

"Anything?" Ed raised his eyebrows, looking amused.

Alec couldn't think of anything he'd refuse Ed right now, but he was still relieved when Ed took Alec's cock in his hand and said, "I'd really like you to fuck me again. I haven't been able to stop thinking about you inside me."

Fucking Ed was well within Alec's comfort zone, and given how many boundaries Alec had already pushed tonight, maybe that was for the best. "Okay," he said. "I can do that."

Ed stroked him, his hand firm and tight as he asked. "How do you want me?"

Alec grabbed Ed's hips and walked him back towards the bed. "Like this." He pushed him down and Ed scooted back, spreading his thighs so Alec could crawl between them. "Perfect."

Now he'd finally got Ed where he wanted him, Alec was in no rush, and Ed seemed to pick up on the change of pace. They kissed lazily, letting their hands roam. Alec mapped out the smoothness of Ed's skin with his palms, and Ed combed his fingers through the rough hair on Alec's chest.

"It feels so good against my nipples," Ed muttered between kisses.

Alec moved lower to tease Ed's nipples with his lips and tongue, loving the way they hardened for him and the way Ed gasped and slid his fingers into Alec's hair as he did it. He worked his way down Ed's torso, over the warm skin of his stomach, down to the cradle of his hips where the skin stretched tight over his hipbones as Ed arched up, spreading his legs wider. Alec looked up at him as he lowered his mouth to Ed's cock and licked, tasting him, smelling his scent, watching the flush on his cheeks as he stared down at Alec.

"Fuck," Ed gasped as Alec finally sucked him, taking him deep for a moment before bobbing back up with a swirl of his tongue. Alec was torn, wanting to keep his mouth on Ed for longer, but suspecting Ed wouldn't last long if he did. He felt like a kid in a playground. He wanted to do all the things at once—fuck him, suck him, eat him out. He moaned around Ed's cock, overwhelmed by the strength of his desire.

Ed made the decision for him. Grabbing the lube and condoms and passing them down to Alec, he said, "Please. Fuck me. I want to come with you inside me." He hooked his hands under his knees and pulled them back.

Alec remembered their first night together, when Ed had lain like this, opening himself up for Alec's cock. Ed had been a stranger then. Now he was so much more.

Alec rolled the condom on first and then squeezed some lube into his palm. He slicked his cock and used his fingers on Ed.

At the first gentle touch on his hole, Ed moaned, pushing against him. The tips of Alec's fingers slipped inside, but Ed shook his head. "Your cock," he said. "Just use your cock."

"You sure?"

"Yes, Alec. Please."

As Alec lined himself up, Ed lay back, watching him with hooded eyes. His cheeks were flushed and his lips pink and shiny from their kisses. With his dirty-blond hair tumbling over one eye, he looked like a debauched angel. When Alec pushed inside in one slow, steady thrust of his hips, Ed moaned, squeezing his eyes shut.

"Okay?" Alec rolled his hips carefully, withdrawing just a little. God, Ed felt amazing. He was tight and hot, and Alec wanted to fuck him into the middle of next week.

"Yes." But there was tension in Ed's voice, and Alec knew he wasn't comfortable yet. He wasn't asking Alec to stop, so Alec kept moving gently, shifting his weight slightly and tilting Ed's legs to see if he could find a better angle.

"Oh yes. Fuck." Ed's eyes flew open. He grabbed Alec's hips and pulled. "Like that, but harder."

"Yeah?" Alec grinned, breathless. He could do harder.

Propping himself up on his forearms, he slammed into Ed, fucking him like he'd been dreaming about ever since their first time. This time it was even better, because it meant something. Alec didn't know what, exactly, and maybe it only meant something that would end in heartache, but at this moment, with Ed under him, moaning and urging him on, Alec didn't care about anything outside this room. He stared into Ed's eyes and their gazes locked. There was so much emotion there—heat and passion, along with something softer that was frightening in its intensity. Alec could see it in Ed's face as much as he could feel it in his own heart. He wondered whether it was written all over his features too, whether Ed could see what Alec saw reflected back at him in a feedback loop of need and want and hopeless longing.

"God, Alec," Ed slid a hand into his hair and tugged Alec down into a messy kiss, and it was almost a relief that Alec could no longer see his face because it was too much.

Everything slowed down again. Desperate urgency became a slow, languid build of pleasure. With Ed's tongue in his mouth and Ed's cock hard between their stomachs, Alec spiralled slowly towards orgasm. He wanted to make Ed come, but he couldn't focus. Ed was like a drug, enhancing his senses and stealing his reason. He was dimly aware of Ed slipping a hand between them, and he felt the bump of Ed's knuckles as he jerked himself off. Wet heat spilled between them, and the sensation of Ed's walls pulsing around him dragged Alec over. He groaned, pulling away from the kiss and burying his face into Ed's shoulder as he came and came, shaking with the force of it.

Alec's brain came back online in fractured pieces. First he noticed the scent of Ed's skin. Next he registered the soft stroke of Ed's fingers on the back of his neck.

"Jesus," Alec murmured, his body limp and useless. "Sorry, am I squashing you?"

"A bit." Ed's voice was warm and husky next to his ear. "But only in a good way."

Alec chuckled. He managed to lift his head and press a kiss to Ed's lips. "I'll move in a minute."

Ed slid his arms around Alec's body and held him close. "No rush."

Alec finally roused himself when his cock started to soften. In danger of losing the condom, he pulled out carefully, knotted it, and tossed it onto the floor. "I'll get it later," he said as he flopped onto his back beside Ed.

Ed snuggled closer and threw an arm over Alec's chest. Alec's heart squeezed, and a rush of emotion took his breath away.

"Will you stay?" Ed asked. "I'm not ready for tonight to be over."

"I could probably go for round two a little later," Alec said lightly. It was easier to keep this about the sex. He wasn't ready to find words for the feelings that tightened his chest and made his heart beat faster.

"Sounds good."

They lay quietly for a while.

Ed stroked his hand over Alec's chest, tracing the shape of his muscles and ribs under the soft dark hair. "You're so gorgeous," he murmured. "It's been killing me, being around you in the office, knowing what you look like naked under those sharp suits of yours."

Alec smiled. "Same. I have to force myself not to keep staring at your arse."

Deep down, Alec knew this wasn't just about sex anymore, not for him, anyway. He thought about how exponentially more difficult it was going to be keeping his feelings for Ed under wraps now he'd had this — this intimacy, the sweetness of this evening. He kissed the top of Ed's head, breathing in his warm, comforting scent, and he wished with all his heart that things were different.

CHAPTER EIGHT

Ed listened to the thump of Alec's heart. He had come drying on his belly, but he didn't want to move. He was afraid that if he left the bed to clean up, the mood would be broken. After five weeks of unbearable sexual tension, antagonism, and then finally a slow drift into something easier between them, he still couldn't believe they'd found their way here.

Even in Ed's wildest fantasies, he hadn't dared to dream of this. Alec's arms around him, Alec kissing his hair, the way Alec had looked at him while he'd thrust into him, like Ed was the centre of his universe. His feelings for Alec were careering out of control, way past the physical, and he didn't think he was alone on that ride. But Alec had made it very clear they only had tonight.

Just one more night.

Ed wasn't sure his heart could stand it. But it was too late now. If they only had tonight, he was damn well going to make the most of it.

The second time they fucked, Ed took charge. Alec had dozed off, and Ed woke him with his mouth on his cock. He sucked him into hardness, tasting musk and salt as Alec swelled against his tongue. Alec brought his hands down to smooth Ed's hair away from his face, and Ed looked up to see his smile.

Ed pulled off so he could grin back. "Round two?"

"I think it could be arranged. What did you have in mind?"

"You can just lie there and look sexy. I'm doing all the work this time."

Alec chuckled. "I can do that."

He put one hand behind his head so he could see better, and Ed admired the dark hair in his armpit and the curve of his bicep. "Yeah. You're excellent at that," he agreed.

Ed rolled the condom onto Alec, lubed him up, and lowered himself onto Alec's cock, inch by decadent inch. He held Alec's gaze as he did it, and there was that expression again. For a poker-faced lawyer, Alec sucked at hiding his feelings in the bedroom. Ed wasn't complaining. He didn't think he'd ever get tired of seeing Alec look at him like that. He pushed away the thought that this was probably the last time it would ever happen. Now wasn't the time to be worrying about the future. The present was too good to ruin.

When he'd taken Alec all the way inside, Ed leaned back a little and stroked his own cock until he was fully hard. Alec watched him, his eyes dark and hungry now. He brought his hands to Ed's thighs and stroked, rubbing the sensitive hairs the wrong way as he slid his hands higher so that his thumbs skimmed Ed's balls. "Are you planning on moving? Or are you just going to sit there and jerk off on me? Because while the view is very pleasant, I wouldn't say no to a little action."

Ed rolled his hips, squeezing his muscles as he lifted himself up, before letting gravity pull him back down. He did it again, and then again. "Like this, you mean?"

"Yeah," Alec said breathlessly, "that's exactly the sort of thing I had in mind."

Ed rode Alec slowly and deliberately, seeking his own pleasure while watching Alec's reactions. What worked for Ed seemed to be working for Alec too. A deep flush spread down Alec's neck, and soon he was moaning, arching up into each downward movement of Ed's. He gripped Ed's hips, trying to take control and make him go faster, so Ed grabbed his wrists and pushed them over his head, pressing them into the pillow. "*No*. I want it slow."

Alec groaned in frustration, but he let Ed hold him down and kiss him for a while. Ed was getting close, but he needed more. Sitting up again he wrapped a hand around his cock. He rode Alec faster, stroking himself as Alec watched. The heat of Alec's gaze rippled through Ed, lighting him up.

"Ed." Alec's voice was rough and the desperate sound of his name on Alec's lips drove Ed higher, closer, right to the edge… and then he was tumbling over into bliss. He cried out as he gripped Alec with his thighs, fighting to stay upright as he came, cock pulsing and spilling over his hand and Alec's stomach.

"Fuck, that was hot." Alec was looking at him like he'd seen God.

"You didn't come yet, did you?" Ed wasn't sure. In the throes of his own orgasm, it had been hard to tell.

Alec shook his head. "Nearly, but not quite."

Ed tried a tentative lift of his hips. He was still sensitive from coming, and he couldn't hold back a hiss as Alec's cock brushed his prostate. It wasn't unpleasant; it was just… a lot. But the expression on Alec's face made the slight discomfort worth it.

"Oh yes," he moaned as Ed found a rhythm and an angle he could handle. "Fuck me."

"I'm working on it." Ed huffed out a breathless chuckle. His thighs ached now and his arse felt stretched and sore, but he wanted it. He wanted to feel the ache the next day, a ghost of their shared pleasure until the physical imprint of their night together faded. He fucked Alec harder. The pain was good because it matched the pain in Ed's heart when he thought about facing Alec in the office on Monday and pretending they were nothing to each other.

Their bodies were slippery with sweat. Alec dug his fingers into Ed's hips so hard they'd probably leave bruises. Ed didn't care. It would be another thing to remember this by.

Alec came with a harsh cry, thrusting up deep into Ed.

Ed didn't come again, but it almost felt as though he did as Alec's cock pulsed inside him. He squeezed his internal muscles, shivering with an echo of his own release. "Yeah," he said, grinning down at Alec, who looked totally wrecked. Covered in sweat and Ed's come, he was a far cry from the perfectly coiffed and expensively dressed boss Ed knew in the office.

Alec's lips softened into a smile that made Ed's heart squeeze. He definitely knew which version of Alec he preferred — although the "sexy boss" version of Alec was hot as fuck too.

"Come here," Alec said.

Ed eased himself off, his limbs protesting. "Ouch." He rubbed at his thigh as he flopped onto his side. "Cramp."

Alec dealt with the condom quickly, then put his arms around Ed and tugged the covers up.

Ed burrowed into his chest, loving the scent of Alec and the solid muscular warmth surrounding him. They lay like that, trading increasingly sleepy kisses, until Alec sighed and rolled away. Ed protested, reaching for him. "Don't go," he said before he had time to think better of sounding so needy.

"I'm not going anywhere, but I need a piss before I crash out," Alec said.

Ed let him go with a huff, but when he heard the sound of water running, he realised he ought to go too—unless he wanted to have to get up again in a few hours, and he really didn't.

He found Alec trying to clean his teeth with a hotel flannel.

"You can use my toothbrush if you want," Ed offered.

"It seemed presumptuous."

"You've had your dick in my arse twice tonight. I think we've graduated to the toothbrush-sharing stage of our r— Whatever." Ed cut himself off quickly with a vague wave of his hand. He didn't think "relationship" was a word Alec would want to hear applied to them.

"Thanks." Alec picked up Ed's toothbrush without further comment.

Ed paused, uncertain for a moment. Then decided that peeing while Alec brushed his teeth was going to have to be acceptable, because he was cold and tired and didn't want to wait.

After they'd both finished with teeth and a half-arsed clean-up, they climbed back into Ed's bed, still naked. They settled naturally on their sides, Alec behind Ed, with an arm possessively around his waist, holding him close.

Ed settled back against him with a satisfied smile. Worry and uncertainty lurked at the edge of his consciousness, but he ignored them. They could wait for the morning.

Ed slept like the dead. Even in an unfamiliar bed with another body beside him, he had no recollection of waking in the night. The next thing he knew, it was morning—admittedly early, because it was still dark outside, but the hotel clock told him it was six. That was the time Ed normally got up for work, so his brain was on a timer to kick into consciousness around then.

He rolled onto his back, stretching his muscles. His dick stirred as he remembered why he was aching all over. *Oh yeah*. It had been totally worth it. Alec was completely still beside him save for the rise of his ribcage, his breathing soft and slow. He was obviously fast asleep.

Afforded the luxury of a lie-in, Ed closed his eyes and let himself sink back into oblivion for a while.

The next time he woke, it was light outside. Alec was still asleep beside him, and Ed rolled onto his side to study him. Dark lashes fanned out on Alec's cheekbones and his jaw was shadowed with morning stubble; his lips were soft and slightly parted as he breathed. Ed could happily watch him for hours, but the clock was ticking towards the time when they had to leave Edinburgh and return to London.

Ed's heart clenched painfully at the thought of that. He wasn't ready to give this up. He had to hope Alec would want to make the most of the last few hours they had together before reality intruded and stripped away the beautiful intimacy they'd shared.

Ed rolled onto his side, putting his arm over Alec's chest. He kissed Alec's shoulder, then his neck, then his jaw.

"Mmmm," Alec hummed. "Ed?"

"Yep." Ed smiled as Alec cranked his eyes open and squinted at him. He breathed a silent sigh of relief as Alec returned his smile and reached for him.

This wasn't over yet, then.

They lay together, kissing with their bodies entwined as slow, lazy, morning arousal grew and thickened between them. It was nothing like the sex they'd had before. There was an innocence and a sweetness to it. It felt like a first time as they kissed and stroked each other to climax. Ed came first, his groans muffled against Alec's neck. Alec followed soon after, adding to the mess between them. Even when they were done, they carried on kissing long after, as though neither of them could bear to stop.

Finally, Ed's stomach interrupted them by rumbling.

Alec pulled away, laughing. "Sounds like someone's hungry."

"Yeah," Ed admitted ruefully. "Damn the need to eat."

"We could order room service breakfast, unless you'd rather go down?"

"Oh, I'd like to go down." Ed waggled his eyebrows suggestively. "So yes, room service sounds good. I want a shower first, though. I feel a bit disgusting."

"Me too."

Alec showered while Ed ordered food, and then Ed took his turn in the bathroom.

When he came out, he found Alec on the phone, dressed only in the black boxers he'd been wearing last night and pacing around the bed with the look of a caged tiger. Ed caught a glimpse of the scars on Alec's back as he turned away, and Ed's stomach lurched when he remembered what had caused them.

Alec's brows were drawn down tight. Ed felt a prickle of anxiety, wondering whether this was work-related drama that might affect him.

Then Alec said, "Don't worry, Mother. I'll be there." There was a short silence. "I'm not sure about Belinda. I'll need to check whether she's free. I'll let you know tomorrow." Another silence. "We're not joined at the hip. It's not that kind of relationship." He caught Ed's gaze and rolled his eyes. Ed smiled in sympathy. "Yes, all right, Mother. See you next weekend." He ended the call with a harassed sigh.

"Sorry," he said to Ed. "She'd already left me two messages while we were still asleep, so I thought it was best to get it over with."

"No worries." Ed didn't like to pry, but Alec filled in the gaps for him.

"It's my father's seventieth birthday party next weekend. I'm expected, obviously, but Mother wants to know whether I'm bringing Belinda. They haven't seen her in a while, and my mother's like a dog with a bone. I think she smells grandchildren." He snorted. "If only she knew. I'll need to bribe Belinda to come with me. She doesn't mind coming to work do's in London, but I don't think she's going to be very keen to travel to Berkshire and stay overnight."

Ed felt a flash of ridiculous jealousy. Belinda wasn't even Alec's real girlfriend, and it wasn't as if Ed actually wanted to go to the party, so why did he care? Alec's family didn't sound like a barrel of laughs. But Ed's traitorous brain couldn't help supplying him with a brief fantasy of being Alec's plus-one, and of what life might be like if they were a real couple.

A loud knock saved Ed from needing to find an appropriate response. He pulled on a hotel robe and went to get the door.

"Hang on," Alec said.

Ed realised Alec was still only in his underwear. He was standing, looking around for something to wear.

"Just get back into bed. I'm sure they've seen it all before." Ed grinned.

When Alec was safely back in bed and his modesty covered by the sheets, Ed let in the girl who was delivering their breakfast. She wheeled in the trolley and unloaded two trays onto the table. She didn't bat an eyelid at Ed in his robe and Alec half-naked and blushing in the bed.

"Thank you," Ed said.

"Thank you, sir. Will there be anything else?"

"No, thanks." There was an awkward pause, and then Ed realised she was expecting a tip. Fuck, he wasn't used to this lifestyle yet. "Oh, um…." He finally located his jeans in a tangled heap on the floor by the bed and pulled out his wallet. He emptied out a handful of coins and gave them to the girl.

"Thanks," she said with a smile before turning to leave.

"Very smooth," Alec teased as the door shut behind her.

"You're a fine one to talk. I saw you cowering in the bed with a face like a tomato."

Alec didn't try to deny it, but a flush darkened his cheeks again as Ed passed him a tray of food and coffee. "It was weird… her seeing us like this," Alec admitted. "Even though she doesn't know who I am and I'm never going to see her again. I'm not used to anyone knowing about me."

"I know." Ed brought the other tray to the bed and took off his robe before climbing back in beside Alec.

They ate in silence. Melancholy descended on Ed like mist. This morning had the feel of an ending, as though something was slipping away from him. But he was losing something he'd never really had in the first place.

When they were finished with breakfast, Alec carried the trays back to the table. Ed was surprised when he got back into bed again. Alec lay down and put his arm over Ed's waist where he sat propped up on the pillows. He pressed his face against Ed's hip, so Ed couldn't see his expression. He felt the gust of Alec's sigh against his skin.

Ed tentatively put his hand in Alec's hair and stroked. Alec stayed where he was, so Ed kept stroking. "When do we have to check out?"

"Too soon." Alec's voice was soft. Then he added wistfully, "I wish we had more time."

Regret was a dull twist in Ed's stomach. "Me too." He scooted down the bed so he could wrap his arms around Alec and hold him tight.

"Ed," Alec said eventually. He drew away, just enough that they could see each other. *His eyes are so beautiful*, Ed thought. The clear hazel pure and compelling. When Alec held his gaze, it was impossible to look away. "I don't want this to be over between us."

Dangerous hope surged, making Ed's heart pound. "But what…? How?"

"I care about you. I want to keep seeing you. I know we're both busy, but we could manage something. It's not ideal with us working together, of course, but when this deal is closed, I can recommend you move to a new team."

The words flowed out of Alec so quickly, Ed could hardly make sense of them. Alec barely paused for breath before continuing.

"You said you want to work in employment law. Perhaps I could have a word with Katherine, see if they have any work for you in that department? I'm sure nobody would think it was odd or suspect anything."

Ed's brain raced, catching up with what Alec was saying and imagining the possibilities, what it might mean for him. For *them*. Maybe it could work?

Alec went on. "We'd need to be discreet, of course. Nobody could know, but we could see each other outside work."

A cold knife sliced through Ed's heart. "Ever? Nobody could *ever* know?" He searched Alec's face for a hint that he might be ready to at least explore the possibility of a future where he didn't have to hide their relationship.

Alec's expression became shuttered. "I don't know. You know how complicated this is for me. Please Ed, give me a chance. Give *us* a chance?"

Fuck.

No matter how much Ed wanted this, he couldn't do it on Alec's terms. It was almost impossible to get the word out, but he forced it past the lump in his throat. "No." Ed felt torn in two. He wanted so much to say yes, but he couldn't. "Alec, I'm sorry."

"Oh."

The word dropped between them like a stone, and the hurt on Alec's face made Ed wince. He realised how his rejection might sound, and at the very least, he owed it to Alec to be honest.

"You need to understand. It's not that I don't want you… that I don't want this." He gestured between them. "You have no idea. I want this so badly it's killing me to say no." Ed took a deep breath. "But I'm out, Alec. For this relationship to have any future, I need to go out in public with you without you being afraid of what people are thinking. I need to be able to introduce you to my friends… to my family. I can't hide. I won't, not even for you." He felt the sting of tears threatening and his voice was strained. "It's not just about the hiding. I need you to be proud of who you are, because if you're not… if you don't accept yourself as a gay man, how can you truly accept me?"

Alec's face was tight and drawn. "I've never felt this way about anyone before. It's all so new. Can't you give me a little time?"

Ed shook his head slowly. "I'm sorry, but I've been there, done that, and I'm not going back in the closet for anyone again. It's too hard. I dated a guy at university who wasn't out, and it was toxic. I felt like a guilty secret, and I can't do that to myself again. His fear of being caught tainted everything. It made our whole relationship feel like something dirty and shameful. I can't live like that."

"I understand," Alec said hoarsely. "It wasn't fair of me to ask you." He rolled away and got out of bed. "I'd better go and pack."

Ed didn't trust himself to speak. Part of him wanted to stop Alec from leaving, to tell him he'd changed his mind, to agree to see Alec in secret and hope it would be enough. Instead, he swallowed the words down and watched in silence as Alec dressed in his clothes from last night.

"I'll meet you down in the lobby," Alec said quietly. "We need to check out in half an hour. I'll call reception and ask them to book us a taxi to take us to the airport."

They sat in silence on the drive to Edinburgh airport. There was nothing to say, and their subdued mood was like a grey blanket weighing them down.

Alec was checking emails on his phone and typing a message to someone. Ed should probably check his inbox too, but he couldn't muster up the energy. Instead he leaned his head against the window and watched the streets flash past. Buildings and cars, people going about their everyday lives. Ed wondered what troubles those people had, what losses they had to bear, what heartbreaks. From the outside you couldn't tell when someone was hurting.

He glanced at Alec, and his face was like the stone of the tenements that lined the streets: hard and forbidding. Once Ed would have been intimidated by Alec when he looked like that, but now he knew him. He knew the humour and the capacity for tenderness that lay behind the harsh exterior. He'd glimpsed the bone-deep loneliness and vulnerability beneath. Regret pressed heavily on Ed's chest. He felt as though his heart might split under the weight of it, though whether it was breaking for himself or for Alec, he wasn't sure.

Alec tried to hide his tension as the plane prepared for take-off, but Ed noticed the way Alec had clenched his fist on his thigh and the way his leg jiggled as the engines got louder.

Ed reached for Alec's hand and wrapped his own around it. Alec tensed, looking around quickly to see if anyone was watching them. They weren't. The only people who could have seen them, even if they had looked, was a young couple across the aisle, and they were far too busy settling a fussy baby on the mother's lap to pay any attention. Ed stroked the back of Alec's hand with his thumb and Alec relaxed, his shoulders dropping slightly.

"Thanks," he murmured.

"I still owe you big for the spider rescue."

Alec gave a wan smile. "Speaking of which, how is your foot today?"

"Better after spending twelve hours in bed. I'll take it easy for the rest of the weekend."

"Good. It's going to be a busy week. I'll need you on your toes on Monday."

In the final run-up to the signing of the purchase agreement later that week, the whole team would be working like maniacs, double-checking every detail so there wouldn't be any last-minute hitches.

"Luckily my toes are fine," Ed said. "But my heel still hurts like a bitch if I put too much weight on it. I hope you won't need me to do too much running around. You might need to find another minion to do coffee and photocopier duty for a couple of days."

Ed kept hold of Alec's hand throughout take-off, and he didn't let go until the seat belt lights went off. The tension between them had eased once more, but Ed was all too aware of how short the flight was. Soon they would touch down in London and this time out from their normal life would be over. Alec was slipping away from him, and Ed had to let him go.

As the plane began its descent, Ed resisted the urge to take Alec's hand again. If Alec wanted it, it would be up to him. Ed could feel the tension rolling off Alec in waves, but Alec only clenched his fist in his lap and kept his gaze fixed on the back of the seat in front.

When the plane touched down and slammed the brakes on, Ed nudged him. "We survived."

Alec's smile was pinched and unhappy. "It appears so."

Once they were in a taxi on their way back to Central London, Alec checked his phone for messages.

"Shit," he muttered as he read something on the screen.

"Everything okay?"

"Belinda's away next weekend, so she can't come to my father's birthday lunch."

"I thought you'd already told your mother she might not be free?"

"I know, but I was hoping she'd be able to make it. It's easier spending time with them when she's around. They love her, and she's a great distraction. It takes the focus off me. Oh well. At least my brother will be there. Apparently he's bringing a girlfriend, so that will keep them happy. He doesn't usually stick with a girl long enough to introduce her to the family."

Alec lapsed back into a preoccupied silence, and Ed didn't have the will to keep the conversation going. No matter how much he wanted to be involved in Alec's life, it wasn't going to happen. He shifted in his seat, and the twinge of his overused muscles reminded him painfully of last night. He pushed the memory away and got out his laptop. He had lots to do before Monday. He might as well start now.

CHAPTER NINE

When Alec got home, his flat felt too big and empty after spending twenty-four hours in Ed's company. So Alec did what he always did and buried himself in work so he didn't have time to feel lonely. He didn't even stop to unpack. He got out his laptop and lost himself in preparations for the final exchange: emailed bullet points of the meeting to the rest of the team and then started making the final changes to the draft purchase agreement ready for the meeting with both parties next week.

Alec only realised he'd skipped lunch when his stomach growled, and when he went to look for something to eat, he found his fridge and cupboards were pathetically bare. He poured himself a bowl of muesli and some milk that was a couple of days past its use-by date but still smelled okay. Sitting on his pristine sofa in his immaculate living room, he was suddenly struck by how empty it was. *It's like a show home*, he thought. *Perfect in outward appearance but devoid of any warmth or comfort.* A depressingly accurate metaphor for his own life.

His thoughts strayed inevitably to Ed, and an aching void opened up in his chest as he remembered their conversation from the morning. Ed had let Alec down so gently. There had been regret written all over his face, so Alec was in no doubt that Ed had feelings for him too. Somehow, instead of being a balm to his pride, the knowledge only made the rejection sting all the more, because Alec knew he had only himself to blame for the fucking mess that was his life. For the first time ever, Alec had met someone who made him want more, someone who made him hope that one day he could have a relationship lasting longer than a few hours. But in order to get to a place where that was possible, Alec had to find the courage to untangle the web of lies his personal life was built on, and in the process he feared he might damage his professional reputation.

Alec's chest tightened and his heart beat fast as fight or flight hormones surged through his bloodstream. The walls were closing in on him, but he couldn't see a way out. Stomach churning, he stared at his bowl of soggy cereal before slamming it down on the glass coffee table with a crash. Crawling out of his skin, there was no way he'd be able to get any more work done today unless he found a way to burn some of this tension off.

He changed into workout clothes and ran to his gym a few streets away. There he put himself through brutal circuits of cardio and weightlifting until every muscle in his body hurt and his legs were like jelly.

Back home he managed to force down some food after a shower, and then got his brain back into work mode. The unhappiness and frustration were still there, but muted now — an irritating background hum rather than a deafening roar.

Alec supposed he'd better get used to it. He had a feeling those emotions weren't going to go away anytime soon.

Alec was already at his desk when Ed arrived in the office on Monday. He steeled himself before looking up and greeting him with a light "Good morning." His heart pounded. He was anything but casual on the inside.

"Hi, Ed," James said from behind his laptop.

"Morning," Ed replied. His blue gaze rested on Alec for a moment before Ed busied himself with getting out his laptop.

There, that wasn't so hard, Alec told himself. If all went well, they'd only be working together for another week or so anyway. Once this deal was closed, chances were Ed would move on to gain experience with a different team, and Alec would be able to breathe again.

Forcing himself to focus on making notes for the morning briefing, Alec wasn't paying attention as other members of the team drifted in and took their seats around him. It wasn't until he heard a loud exclamation from Jen that he realised most of the others were clustered around Maria's desk. She had her laptop open, and people were admiring something on the screen.

"They're such a handsome couple," Jen said. "And they look so in love."

"They are." Maria smiled. "It was a lovely wedding."

"I've never been to a gay wedding." James sounded put out. "Ed, if you ever get married, will you invite me?"

Ed chuckled. "Sure, James. You'll be top of my guest list, as long as you promise to save a dance for me."

Alec's stomach flip-flopped like a fish. He felt sudden intense envy for Ed and his honesty. He made being out look so easy, when for Alec his orientation was this huge, shameful secret he'd hidden for years. Ed was going to be able to have his career without needing to lie about his life and relationships. Maybe, if Alec had been brave earlier, he could have had that too. But he'd dug himself into a hole where the sides were so steep he couldn't see what lay outside—unless he could find the courage to try climbing out.

Alec realised he was being antisocial and was in danger of attracting unwanted attention, so he made himself get up and approach Maria's desk. "Can I see?" he asked.

The others parted to make space for him, Ed on his left and Jen on his right, and he found himself staring at a photo of two men in dark suits. They were facing each other, their hands clasped between them, and they gazed into each other's eyes as if nobody else existed in the world.

Alec tried to think of an appropriate comment, but he floundered, half-formed platitudes sticking in his throat. Maria clicked through to the next photo, which showed the same couple on a dance floor, kissing each other while a crowd of people looked on, smiling and clapping.

Katherine's voice from behind Alec's shoulder made him start; he hadn't realised she'd come in. "Oh, what a beautiful photo."

The warmth in her voice prodded at the sore spaces inside Alec. He was denying himself that acceptance because he wouldn't even try to be honest.

Trapped by the people around him, Alec couldn't move away without making it into an issue. So he was forced to watch as Maria scrolled through several more pictures. Achingly aware of Ed beside him, close enough to touch, Alec gritted his teeth and pasted a closed-lipped smile onto his face. He hummed sounds of approval and hoped nobody would notice his inner turmoil.

Finally he was saved when Maria closed the photo window and turned. "Sorry, Alec. I just realised we've gone past the time for the briefing. I'll stop distracting us with my brother's wedding photos." She smiled up at him.

"No problem," Alec said, but the group was already breaking up, ready to work. "Okay, let's adjourn to the breakout room."

In the final week running up to the signing of the purchase agreement, the workload was intense. Every last detail had to be checked and double-checked. The whole team worked twelve-hour days and were also burning the midnight oil at home.

Alec and Ed only interacted on a professional level, but every time Alec let his guard slip and memories of their weekend together crept into his consciousness, he was assaulted by a longing so intense it took his breath away like a kick to the stomach.

On Friday morning they assembled in the office ready to take the car over to their client's offices for the final face-to-face exchange, arranged at Mackenzie's insistence. Alec was going with Katherine, who had invited Ed to come along for the ride.

Ed looked particularly handsome this morning. He was wearing a beautifully cut suit Alec hadn't seen before, and his blue tie brought out his eyes.

For a fleeting moment, Alec allowed himself a fantasy where he pulled Ed towards him by that tie and pushed him to his knees, messing up Ed's perfectly coiffed hair with his fingers while Ed sucked him into oblivion.

"The car's waiting downstairs," Jen said, snapping Alec's attention back to the present like a rubber band.

Adrenaline and anticipation rippled through Alec in a heady rush. There was nothing like the feeling of a deal done, of closure after weeks of negotiation and work. It was intensely satisfying. Right until the last minute, there was always the fear that something could go wrong and bring everything crashing down around them. Another hour and, God willing, it would be in the bag.

Ed looked nervous in the car on the way over. He jiggled his leg, and Alec wanted to put his hand on it to still it.

"Calm down, Ed. It's going to be fine," he said instead. "If you go in there looking nervous, it will unsettle our client."

Ed flushed. "Sorry. I didn't even realise I was fidgeting. Feel free to kick me if I do it in the meeting."

Katherine chuckled. "This really is a formality, Ed. It's rare for anything to go wrong at this stage, especially when both parties want the sale. Mackenzie was looking to sell and is happy with the deal we've negotiated. The team has done well."

"Alec's a slave driver." Ed grinned. "But he knows how to get things done. It's been a great experience working under him."

Alec glanced at Ed, wondering whether that was a deliberate innuendo or a Freudian slip, but Ed didn't seem to notice what he'd said.

"Alec has done an excellent job with this deal," Katherine replied. "His team was a great place for you to gain some experience, Ed. I'm sure you've learned a lot."

Alec hoped they'd assume his flush was due to Katherine's praise rather than Ed's choice of words.

When they reached the hotel offices, they were ushered straight into a meeting room. Maxwell greeted them with warm handshakes and a broad smile. If he had any exchange-day jitters, he hid them well.

"Mackenzie and his people are about ten minutes away, then it's all systems go."

Much to Alec's relief, the meeting went without a hitch. Once they'd signed and witnessed the purchase agreement, the mood in the room changed from thick tension to happy exhilaration. There was more handshaking and exchanging of pleasantries. Coffee was served, and Alec worked his way around the room thanking the Scottish legal team for their hard work and congratulating both parties on the sale. "So, Mr Mackenzie, do you have plans for how to spend your retirement?"

"Travelling," the older man answered with a smile. "My wife's been on at me for years to see more of the world. So hotels will still be a big part of my future, only staying in luxury ones in faraway places rather than running my own."

"That sounds good. I hope you enjoy it."

"I'm sure I will," Mackenzie said warmly. "Thank you again."

"You're welcome."

Katherine called Alec into her office shortly before the end of the day. Alec had spent the afternoon tying up a few loose ends of paperwork, but he'd been struggling to concentrate, still buzzed and elated after the events of the morning.

"Are you still on cloud nine?" she asked as he took a seat opposite her. "It always takes me a while to come down."

"It's a good feeling." He nodded. "But I'm already looking forward to the next one. What are you going to give me to tackle this time?"

"There's a retail chain acquisition in the pipeline that we'll be pulling a team together for soon. But that's not what I wanted to talk to you about." There was a smile on her face.

Alec raised his eyebrows, heart kicking up a notch as he tried to keep his voice casual. "Oh yes?"

"You're going to get an invitation to a meeting with the board to discuss the outcome of your partner application next week. I don't know for sure what the decision is yet, but I know you've impressed them, and your work on this deal was a big factor. I think your chances are good."

Alec stared at her. A smile spread across his face and excitement rose as her words sank in. This was it. This was what he'd been working towards for years, and he was so close to getting what he wanted. He didn't dare let himself hope too hard. "Thank you," he finally managed.

"You deserve it, Alec. I only told them what I believe. You'll be an asset to the firm. They'd be mad *not* to offer it to you, in my opinion."

"Thank you," he said again. From Katherine, that meant a lot. She gave praise sparingly, so it was all the more precious when it came.

"There's nothing to thank me for. Now go and take your team out for a drink, they've earned it. I'll talk to you next week about the new deal."

"Will do. Have a good weekend, Katherine." Alec stood and was about to leave when Katherine spoke again.

"Oh, I almost forgot. How did Ed perform on the team? From what I saw, he did well."

"He did." Alec flushed, hoping his expression wouldn't betray his feelings. He tried to tamp them down and regain his objectivity. Ed was good at his job, and Alec wasn't about to fuck it up for him. "He's got a lot of potential. He's thorough, hardworking, and was a valuable member of the team."

"Do you want to keep him on for the next deal? It's your call. If he's valuable to you, then you could keep him on, or even encourage him to apply for a permanent position."

Alec hesitated. If he seemed too keen to let Ed go, it wouldn't look good for Ed, but his life would be easier if Ed were in a different department. "Well, he's been an asset. But I happen to know his ambitions lie in employment law. Perhaps you could put in a word for him and see whether they have any work for him over there?"

"Okay." Katherine nodded. "That makes sense. Maybe we can move him over to Employment. They have a sexual harassment case brewing that looks like it's going to be a big one. They're putting a team together for that at the moment, I believe. I'll make some calls and see what I can do."

Alec felt a weight lift off his shoulders. Much as he'd miss the day-to-day contact with Ed, it would be easier this way. Alec couldn't do his job if he was pining like a lovesick schoolboy. He'd get over Ed faster if he didn't have to share an office space with him. When Ed was in the room, it was as though there wasn't enough oxygen left for Alec. "Sounds good. Thanks. I'm sure he'll appreciate it."

"Right, Alec. Go and celebrate, and take some time to relax this weekend. You've earned it."

If only, Alec thought. With his father's birthday party hanging over his head like an axe, he feared his weekend would be far from relaxing. But he replied smoothly. "Will do. Thanks, Katherine. I'll see you on Monday."

Friday-night drinks were extra raucous that night. The culmination of weeks of painstaking work had put them in the mood for celebration. The first round was champagne, on Alec, and the three bottles he'd bought for the six of them to share didn't last long.

James offered to buy the next round. "I warned Emily I'd be late tonight. I have a free pass, and she even promised to get up with Charlotte in the morning. I have a scheduled hangover, and I'm going to make the most of it." He seemed well on the way already. His eyes glittered and his cheeks were flushed.

Alec was drinking slowly, spinning out his second glass of champagne and making it last. Partly because he didn't trust himself to be around Ed if he was drunk, and partly because the last thing he needed when dealing with his parents was to be feeling under par. He found spending time with them difficult enough at the best of times.

Ed wasn't drinking much either. He'd accepted a drink from James, but after that he switched to lemonade when the others ordered a round of cocktails.

Maria asked Ed about his weekend plans.

"I'm going home to see my family," Ed replied. "I haven't seen them since Christmas because I've been so busy with work. My littlest sisters have been pestering me relentlessly via iMessage for the last couple of weeks. I can't take the emoji-induced guilt anymore, so I've given in." Ed smiled. "Seriously, though, I can't wait to see them all."

Alec wondered what it must feel like to have a family that made you smile when you thought about visiting them.

The party started to break up around half past nine, with Maria making her excuses first, followed by Jon and Jen.

"But the night is young!" James protested, waving his glass a little wildly and slopping whatever he was currently drinking onto the floor. James had been working his way down the cocktail menu and was rather the worse for wear. "You chaps aren't going to desert me, are you?" He made puppy eyes at Alec and Ed. "Stay for another?"

Alec met Ed's amused gaze. Ed shrugged. "I don't need to rush off."

Alec wanted an early night, but looking into the clear blue of Ed's eyes and seeing the smile curving those familiar lips, he couldn't bring himself to leave.

"You twisted my arm," Alec said to James. His glass was empty, so he caught the eye of one of the servers and they placed their orders.

James ordered yet another cocktail and didn't seem to notice or care that Alec and Ed both ordered soft drinks.

"I'm going to wring out a kidney," James got up, wobbling unsteadily. Alec put out a hand to stop him lurching into the table and watched as he wove his way towards the toilets.

Ed laughed once he'd gone. "Someone's going to be feeling rough in the morning."

"Yes." Alec shook his head ruefully. "He doesn't usually drink much, so he's not used to it." He picked up James's glass, which was still half-full of orange liquid. "Do you think he'll notice if this disappears?"

"I doubt it."

Alec took a sip of the potent mixture and wrinkled his nose. "Ugh. I was going to try and save him from himself, but this is disgustingly sweet. I think it involves peach schnapps. Can you stomach it?" He offered the glass to Ed, who took it, looking dubious.

Ed sniffed it, but that was as far as he got. "God, it's definitely got peach schnapps in it. So that would be a no from me." Before Alec realised what Ed was doing, Ed poured the disgusting concoction into a large potted plant that stood beside their table. "Best place for it."

"Poor plant." Alec laughed. "It will probably kill it."

Ed shrugged. "Better the plant than James. It will be a miracle if he makes it home without throwing up in the taxi as it is."

The next round arrived just as James got back from the toilet. He picked up his new drink — luckily he seemed to have forgotten the existence of the one they'd disposed of.

"I'll probably regret this in the morning," he said before taking a huge slurp.

Alec thought he was going to regret it rather sooner than the morning, but he kept that to himself.

By the time they'd finished the final round of drinks, James was practically falling asleep on the table. "Sorry," he mumbled. "It's not jus' the booze. Late nights and early mornings… you know how it is."

Alec patted him on the shoulder sympathetically. He knew the strains of the job only too well, and he didn't have an early-rising toddler to add into the equation. "Let's get you into a taxi and send you home to Emily."

James nodded owlishly, his head propped up on one hand.

"Where do you live, James?" Ed asked.

"Stoke Newington."

"That's on the way out to where I live. I'll share a cab with you."

"You sure?" Alec asked him quietly. James's eyes had slipped closed; he was past paying much attention to the conversation around him.

"It's probably for the best. I'm not sure he'll make it home otherwise. James, what street and what number?" Ed nudged James until he opened his eyes and mumbled out his address while Ed typed it into his phone.

They supported James out of the bar. He could barely walk now. With one arm around each of their shoulders, they practically carried him down the road to the taxi rank.

"I'll come with you," Alec said, shifting James's dead weight. "He's completely out for the count. You'll never be able to get him to his own front door."

"But it's in the wrong direction for you. You'll be miles from home."

"That's what taxis are for." Alec sighed.

"Good thing they pay you well."

"I should claim this on expenses. Katherine told me to take my team out and celebrate. Though I'm not sure she had this level of celebration in mind."

Ed laughed. "Celebration or drunken debauchery. There's a fine line."

When they made it to the front of the queue, another black London taxi pulled up within minutes. The cabbie frowned when he saw the state of James. "He's not gonna throw up, is he, mate? Because there's a clean-up charge if he does."

"He'll be fine," Alec assured him. He wished he were as confident as he sounded.

Miraculously, they made it to James's house without mishap. James slept the whole way, his head back and mouth hanging open, seated between them. Alec asked the driver to wait while they manhandled James out of the back of the car. The sudden shock of cold air after the warmth of the cab woke James up a little and he managed to stand, albeit unsteadily.

"Where are we? Oh!" The surprise on his face at realising he was on his own doorstep was comical. He fumbled around in his pocket for his key but couldn't manage to line it up in the lock, so

Ed did it for him. Finally the door opened and James staggered in with one hand on the wall for support. Alec glanced inside to check whether there was another locked door he needed to get through, but it looked as though James lived in a maisonette that had its own front door, which they'd just passed through. There was a light on in the hallway, and Alec saw a shoe rack and a line of coats on hooks, including one small pink one. They were in the right place, then; their duty done as far as Alec was concerned.

"Night, James," Alec said. Then he closed the door behind James and made sure it locked.

He turned to Ed. "Your place next, then, if it's close to here? And then I'll get the driver to take me all the way back to Pimlico."

"Okay." Ed yawned, covering his mouth.

James obviously wasn't the only one who'd been short on sleep this week.

Back in the taxi, there was a space between them where James had been. Alec desperately wanted to slide over, to take Ed's hand or put an arm around him. But Ed wasn't his to touch, and he didn't have the right. For the first time in the weeks that he'd known Ed, Alec had a glimmer of hope. Next week he was getting the promotion he'd been waiting for. Maybe once he'd got the job, he could begin to dismantle the mess of lies and omission around his personal life.

"We probably won't be working together now this deal is over," Alec said.

Ed turned his head to look at him. "Oh?"

"Katherine asked me, and I recommended they move you to a different department." Ed's brow furrowed, so Alec added hastily, "Not because you did a bad job, far from it. I told her the truth. You did really well. But she's going to see whether they have anything for you in Employment. I know that's where you'd prefer to be working, anyway."

"Oh, wow. That's great, thank you." Ed said, and then he gave a small smile. "I suppose it's probably for the best... for other reasons too."

"Exactly." Alec didn't elaborate. The other reasons were making him want to pull Ed into his lap in the back of this taxi right then.

They fell silent, and Alec couldn't help wondering whether Ed's mind had gone to the same place his had — to that hotel room in Scotland and the night they'd spent together. His yearning for Ed was so strong it was hard to resist, but Ed had made it very clear it was over between them. Alec couldn't blame him, and in a weird, twisted way, he was glad. Ed deserved better. Alec didn't want to drag Ed into his lonely closet.

His heart heavy, Alec let his head fall back against the headrest and allowed the exhaustion of the week to overwhelm him. He closed his eyes and his thoughts drifted, lulled by the hum of the engine.

When the taxi lurched to a stop, Alec sat up, blinking. He'd dozed off, and for a moment he'd forgotten where he was.

"This is where I get out." Ed got a twenty pound note out of his pocket and tried to give it to Alec, who waved it away. "No, take it. It's for my share of the taxi. It's going to cost you a fortune to get all the way back to your place from here as it is."

"James will chip in on Monday, I'm sure." Alec took the money anyway. He sensed Ed's pride would make him argue, and the longer the driver had to wait, the more the numbers ticked over on the meter.

"Goodnight." Ed hesitated for a moment, and then he put his hand on Alec's leg and squeezed. "Good luck with your dad's birthday thing tomorrow."

"Thank you," Alec said, touched that Ed had remembered. "I hope you have fun with your family." Ed's face registered surprise, so Alec added, "I heard you talking to Maria about it earlier. Have a good weekend, Ed. I'll see you on Monday."

Ed smiled before patting Alec's knee and removing his hand. "Thanks. Bye."

"Where to next, mate?" The cabbie asked as Ed got out.

"Pimlico."

As the taxi pulled away from the kerb, Alec closed his eyes again. Ed's smiling face floated into his imagination. Until recently, Alec had always thought of his flat as a sanctuary. Peace and solitude away from the noise and bustle of the rest of his life. Now it felt as though he were heading towards an isolation chamber. He wished he could have asked Ed to come home with him, but surely Ed would have refused. Alec sighed. For once he was grateful for the bone-deep tiredness at the end of the working week. He'd have no trouble sleeping tonight, no matter how miserable he was feeling.

CHAPTER TEN

Ed was up bright and early on Saturday morning. He'd been too tired to pack before he went to sleep the night before, so he had to hurry now. He showered, had breakfast, dressed, and brushed his teeth, packing a few things into an overnight bag as he went. He hadn't booked a train ticket, so it didn't matter too much what time he got to the station, but he wanted to try and get home as early as possible so he could spend the maximum amount of time with his family.

He made it to Victoria Station shortly after half nine and was on a train by ten. He texted his mum to let her know what time he'd be getting in and told her he'd get a taxi so he wouldn't need a lift from the station. Ed settled back with his earbuds in, listening to Vampire Weekend as the train carried him south, towards the coast and home.

As always, in the moments when his mind had time to wander, Ed found himself thinking of Alec. Regret tugged in the space below Ed's ribs, like a fish hook trying to reel him in. He replayed that final conversation they'd had in the hotel for the umpteenth time in his head, wondering again whether he'd made the right choice. Then he sighed, closing his eyes and letting his head rest against the cool window pane. Deep down he knew he'd done the right thing, despite how difficult it had been to turn Alec down. Ed couldn't be in a relationship with Alec while he was in the closet, no matter how much Ed wanted him.

Ed's train pulled into Worthing an hour and a half later. He went through the ticket barriers and was heading for the main doors with his bag on his shoulder, earbuds still blasting music, when he was knocked sideways by two small bodies slamming into him with no warning. They tackle-hugged him, screaming his name so loudly he could hear them even over the music.

"Blimey." He steadied himself with a hand on one small blonde head, pulling his earbuds out. "You guys nearly gave me a heart attack!"

He put his bag down and crouched so he could hug his sisters properly.

"Did you see my hair, Ed? Look! Isn't it awesome?" Alice drew back and waved the tips of her hair at him. They'd been dip-dyed bright red.

"And look at mine too!" Ava demanded. Hers was dark blue where Alice's was red. "Which do you like best?"

"I think they both look brilliant," Ed answered diplomatically. He had years of experience at refereeing twin rivalry and knew better than to encourage it. "I bet your teachers are glad you had different colours. It'll make it easier for them to tell you apart."

"We're on holiday next week, and it will have mostly washed out before we go back to school," Alice said. "That's the only reason Mummy did it. In the Easter holidays, I'm going to do mine purple and Ava's going to do hers green."

"Or maybe turquoise. I haven't decided yet."

"You said green."

"I can change my mind."

Alice frowned and put her hands on her hips. "But you can't do purple because I bagged purple."

Ed laughed, standing up to finally greet his mum, who was waiting patiently, a smile on her face as the twins carried on bickering.

"Hi, sweetheart." She opened her arms and wrapped him up in a hug that warmed him down to his toes.

"Hi, Mum." He hugged her back hard, his nose in her hair, an ash version of the twins' blonde. "You didn't need to come and meet me. But thanks."

"It's no trouble." She released him, and Ed stooped to pick up his bag. "Anyway, I think Alice and Ava would have exploded if they'd had to wait any longer to see you. They've been looking forward to it all week."

Their argument over hair forgotten, the twins were now fighting over who got to hold Ed's free hand.

"Shall I take that for you?" His mum grinned, holding out her hand for his bag.

Ed chuckled. "I think you'd better."

With peace restored, the twins tugged on his hands as they led him towards the car, both chattering away non-stop.

In the car, with the twins in the back, Ed's mum could get a word in again.

"So, how are you?" she asked. "You look tired. Are they working you too hard?"

"Depends on your definition of too hard, I suppose." Ed was pretty sure his mum wouldn't approve of the hours he'd been putting in since he started at Baker Wells. "But you know it goes with the job. This is what I want to do, so it's worth it."

"Hmmm. I suppose."

Ed got the feeling she had a lot more that she wanted to say, but he appreciated that she kept her thoughts to herself. His mum had always been supportive; thrilled for him when he'd done well at uni and even more so when he'd landed this job. She worried too, but Ed knew it was only because she loved him.

"How's Gemma?" he asked. "Too cool to come and meet her brother at the station?"

His mum laughed. "Maybe a little. She was busy baking when we left—while simultaneously talking to a friend on FaceTime—so she couldn't have come even if she'd wanted to."

"Gemma's got a boyfriend," Alice announced from the back seat. "He's called Zac."

Ava chimed in. "Yeah, she spends *all day* texting him."

"Sounds serious." Ed glanced at his mum, who was smiling.

"Young love these days mostly seems to involve texting and messaging each other on Instagram. They don't see each other much out of school—which is fine by me." She chuckled. "Speaking of boyfriends…." She trailed off hopefully.

Ed groaned. "Mum."

"Oh, come on, you know I keep hoping you'll meet someone."

"I don't have time for relationships," Ed said evasively. It was almost true. He certainly didn't have the energy to go looking for someone to distract him from Alec, even if he'd wanted to.

"That's a shame." His mum sounded disappointed.

Back at the house, Gemma flung her arms around Ed as she greeted him. "Hey," she said.

"Blimey, Gem. You've grown again." Ed looked her up and down when she pulled away. She must have shot up at least another inch since he'd seen her at Christmas, just a few weeks ago.

"Well, obviously." She rolled her eyes, but the pleased flush on her cheeks gave her away.

Greg, Ed's stepdad, stood up from his seat at the kitchen table. "Hi, Ed. Good to see you."

"You too." Ed moved forward to give him a quick hug.

Greg was the only father he'd ever really known. Ed's dad had left when he was five, and he hadn't seen him since he was seven. Greg had come into Ed's and his mum's lives at around the same time. Greg had filled the space Ed's biological father had left behind, loving Ed unconditionally and never making him feel he was less important than his sisters.

"What's cooking?" Ed sniffed. The smell of baking permeated the warm air in the kitchen.

"Double choc chip muffins."

"Awesome." Ed turned to his mum. "Shall I put my bag upstairs? I assume I'm in my old room. You haven't turned it into a gym or a man cave for Greg yet?" The twins liked sharing, so Ed's bedroom had remained nominally his when he went away to uni, even though most of his stuff was in the flat in London now.

Greg laughed. "I should be so lucky."

"You've got your shed. What more do you need?" Ed's mum teased. Then she turned back to Ed. "And yes, it's still the same in there. I made up the bed for you."

"Thanks, Mum."

Ed carried his bag upstairs, smiling as the fourth step creaked as it always had. He opened the door to his room and was assaulted by memories.

He looked at the desk, where he'd sweated blood revising for his A levels, the narrow bed where he'd lain and fantasised about David Beckham for years, and where he'd eventually had his first awkward, fumbling hand job from Jeremy who lived up the street and was in the year above him at school. The walls were still painted in the too-dark shade of blue he'd insisted on when he was thirteen and the duvet cover was the Harry Potter one he'd got for his sixteenth birthday — a joke gift from his mum that had ended up being his favourite. She still always put it on when he came to visit. It made Ed smile.

Ed sat on the edge of the bed and ran his hand over the cover. Quiet contentment filled him as he relaxed properly for the first time in weeks. Some things never changed. The girls got bigger, Greg and his mum got a few extra laugh lines, but home still felt like home.

It was good to be here.

Alec enjoyed the drive out to Newbury despite his trepidation. Living in Central London, he rarely used his car. It was an expensive luxury he could probably have done without, but he kept it anyway. What was the point of working the hours he did if you couldn't enjoy some of the perks of the salary?

When he finally escaped the snarl of London traffic and hit a clear stretch on the M4, he settled back behind the wheel of his Saab and put his foot down.

The place his mother had booked for lunch was a new restaurant that Alec had never been to before. It was a purpose-built extension on the back of a country pub. According to his mother, it had rave reviews. No doubt it would be good. His family never settled for anything but the best.

Alec was heading straight there rather than meeting his parents at their house. That would mean he'd need to stay sober so he could drive his car back to their house later, but it postponed the family-only part of the day, and Alec was all for delaying that as long as possible. With the buffer of the other guests, the lunch would be all about keeping up appearances. Alec was good at playing the part of the dutiful son. He had years of practice.

He arrived a few minutes after twelve — the time his mother had told him to be there for pre-lunch drinks. Alec paused for a moment, gripping the wheel, and took a deep breath as he shifted gears in his brain ready to deal with his family. He found them exhausting. All perfect etiquette and genteel veneer on the surface, with a mess of ugly dysfunctionality lurking underneath. He fleetingly wondered what Ed would make of them.

"Alec, darling."

His mother was the first to spot him as he entered the building. The restaurant had been set up with one long table to one side for the occasion, and the guests were currently filling the open space beside it, chatting with drinks in their hands.

"Hello, Mother. This looks lovely. Good choice." Alec kissed her cheek, smelling expensive perfume and face powder. It was a social embrace, and there was no real affection in it. Alec couldn't remember the last time his mother had actually hugged him.

"Oh, you brought a gift. Let me take that for you."

Alec handed over the wrapped box, containing a bottle of Chivas Regal whisky for his father. It was hardly an original present, but at least he knew it wouldn't go to waste. "I'd better go and greet the birthday boy," he said.

His father was over by the window chatting with some people Alec recognised as ex-colleagues from his father's legal days. Retired now, his father had been a highly regarded barrister before becoming a judge during his last years in the legal profession.

Alec picked up a glass of champagne from a tray set out on a table as he made his way across the crowded room.

His father saw him coming and raised a hand in greeting. The group around him parted to admit Alec.

"Many happy returns, Father." Alec greeted him with a handshake, as was their wont. He grinned. "You're looking good, barely a day over sixty-nine."

"Alec," his father said as the group around him chuckled. "Good to see you. How are you?"

"I'm well, thank you."

They went through the usual social dance of polite chit-chat, superficial and scripted, with no surprises.

"How's life in corporate?" Edgar, one of his father's contemporaries, asked. "Still enjoying it? No regrets about taking that direction?"

"Not at all." Alec smiled through gritted teeth.

His father had put a lot of pressure on him to follow in his footsteps. He'd wanted Alec to be a carbon copy of himself, but Alec's interest lay in finance and mergers rather than criminal law. He'd always known that was the field he wanted to work in, much to his father's irritation.

"Are you a partner yet?" Edgar asked.

Alec remembered the meeting next week and his heart thumped hard. "I'm working on it."

"Can I have your attention, please?" Alec's mother's voice rose over the crowd and she tapped on her glass with a fork to cut through the chatter. "Don't worry, I don't have a long speech planned." She smiled, all perfect teeth and immaculate lipstick, but the laugh lines that should have enhanced her expression were absent—blitzed away by Botox, no doubt. "I want to propose a toast to Giles, my husband. Three score years and ten today." She raised her glass to him. "Happy birthday, darling. May there be many more."

A murmur of assent followed as the guests raised their glasses obediently.

"Thank you." Alec's father acknowledged the attention with a nod. "I appreciate you all being here to help me celebrate."

"They're ready to serve the starters now," Alec's mother cut back in. "So please take your seats."

There was a seating plan, so Alec went to look at the picture to see where he'd been placed. A little way down the table, near his brother, by the look of it. Alec hadn't seen Caspar yet. He scanned the room. No, there was definitely no sign of his wayward brother. That was bloody typical. Their mother would be livid.

As they took their seats, Alec saw her glaring at the empty spaces. She caught his eye and raised her eyebrows in question, as if Alec might know something. He shrugged. He wasn't his brother's keeper. They'd never been close and rarely had any contact between family gatherings.

Caspar arrived halfway through the starter. He burst in with a stunningly pretty girl on his arm. Well, a woman, really, Alec supposed, but she looked awfully young, with a blonde waterfall of hair and a dress that showed off her model figure. All eyes in the room turned to them.

"I'm terribly sorry we're late," Caspar said loudly. "We got stuck behind a damn horse box doing about fifteen miles an hour down the country lanes, so I tried to take a different route, and then we got lost."

He went to greet his parents first, introducing the girl as Serena. Serena smiled and shook hands with them before they made their way down the table to their seats opposite Alec.

Alec stood to greet him and offered his hand across the table. "Caspar, making an entrance as usual, I see."

"Some things never change." Caspar's smile was broad and genuine and Alec couldn't help smiling back. Life was never boring with his brother around.

He lowered his voice to murmur, "I thought Mother was going to have kittens when she saw your empty seat."

Caspar chuckled. "I bet. Alec, meet Serena. Serena, this is my big brother, Alec."

Close up she was even more beautiful. Alec took her small, smooth hand in his. "It's good to meet you, Serena." And it was good, although surprising, to actually get to meet a girlfriend of Caspar's. They rarely lasted longer than a week. Caspar was a fashion photographer with a penchant for dating the girls he photographed. None of them seemed to hold his interest for long.

"You too." Her grip was strong and sure, and she met his gaze with a smile that would probably make any straight man's knees go weak. "Caspar's told me a lot about you."

"He has?" Alec raised an eyebrow. "All good, I hope."

"Absolutely. I'm a law student, you see, so I was interested to hear about what you do. Tell me, how do you find it working in M&A? I want to work in corporate law eventually… if everything works out." A shadow passed over her beautiful face. "How did you get into it?"

Pleasantly surprised at the turn the conversation had taken, Alec talked about his job and answered Serena's avid questions. She clearly knew her stuff.

Caspar grinned at Alec when there was a gap in the conversation. "I finally found one with brains as well as beauty—*ouch*!" He yelped as Serena nudged him hard in the ribs. "That was supposed to be a compliment."

"Not to any of your exes, it wasn't, and it makes you sound like a sexist pig."

"I *am* a sexist pig."

"If you really were, we wouldn't be together. So stop acting like one."

Alec laughed. "Nice to see someone's seen through him at last."

Chastised, Caspar shook his head, smiling ruefully. "Old habits die hard."

"So, when do you qualify?" Alec asked Serena. "If you're thinking about applying to Baker Wells, let me know. I can put in a good word for you."

"Oh, not for ages yet. I'm only in my first year."

"Oh." Alec shot a glance at Caspar, who flushed. Well, at least she was legal, Alec supposed, even if she was probably still a teenager. She certainly gave the impression of being more mature than most first-year law students were.

"Sorry." Serena winced and put a hand on Caspar's arm. "I'm talking too much."

"Alec's the least of our worries. We've got my parents to deal with," Caspar replied. "But let's save the drama for later."

Alec frowned. Lowering his voice, he leaned closer to Caspar to ask, "What's going on?"

"Long story," Caspar muttered. "You'll find out once the rest of the guests have gone."

The plan was to go back to their parents' house later for a quiet family dinner. Alec had agreed to stay over, and he presumed Caspar had too.

After that little exchange, Alec watched Serena and Caspar carefully during the rest of the meal. Their affection seemed genuine. He'd never seen his brother look so smitten before. He also treated Serena with a respect that was new. His previous girlfriends had been trophies rather than partners, but this was real. Serena seemed happy too. She was warm and genuine but didn't take any shit from Caspar, and Alec admired her all the more for that.

However, despite their obvious love for each other, there was tension there too. Caspar kept glancing nervously at their parents and squeezing Serena's hand reassuringly. Alec wondered what the drama Caspar had promised would consist of exactly.

CHAPTER ELEVEN

They drove back to the family home in two cars. Caspar had been drinking, but Serena had stuck to mineral water, so she slipped in behind the wheel of Caspar's flashy Porsche with his keys in her hand and a smile on her face.

Alec's parents had got a taxi to the restaurant, so Alec offered to drive them. His back seat was wider and more comfortable than Caspar's.

"See you back at the house," Alec said to Caspar.

"Alec, wait." Caspar came close and spoke quietly. "I could use your backup when we get home. I don't have time to explain now. I should have told you before, but—" He looked over Alec's shoulder to where their father was helping their mother into Alec's car. "—the last few weeks have been a little crazy."

Alec frowned. "You're not giving me much of a clue here, Caspar."

"Yeah, I know I'm being cryptic. It's nothing bad, quite the opposite in fact. I'm just not sure how Mum and Dad will take it."

"What's the worst they could do?" That was a question Alec had often asked himself when he considered coming out to them.

"Cut me out of their will?" Caspar grinned. "I earn enough that it wouldn't be the end of the world. I hate pissing them off, though. You know how it is."

Alec knew exactly how it was. "I've got your back," he said. Although he and Caspar weren't particularly close as adults, they'd always covered for each other when they were younger.

"Okay, thanks. See you at the house."

Alec got into his car and turned the key, making the engine purr.

"Caspar's new girl seems charming," his father said as Alec reversed out of the spot.

"She does," his mother agreed. "She looks terribly young, though. I assume she's another of those model types. I wish he'd settle down with someone a bit more suitable. He's thirty now — it's about time."

Alec gripped the steering wheel tightly. Ignoring the pointed remark that was clearly directed at him as much as Caspar, he said lightly, "She's actually a law student." Caspar might not thank him for giving a clue to Serena's age, but at least his parents would respect her for her career choice. "I was talking to her about it over lunch. She's very bright."

"Oh. Well, good for her," his father said, sounding begrudgingly impressed. "Maybe there's more to her than meets the eye, then."

Alec bit his tongue. His father's judgemental attitudes had long been a source of friction between them.

"What about you, Alec?" his mother asked. "We were sorry you couldn't bring Belinda. She's such a lovely girl."

"She's not a 'girl,' Mother." Alec bit back a smile as he imagined Belinda rolling her eyes. "And she sent her apologies, but she's incredibly busy with work at the moment."

His mother sighed theatrically. "Young women these days, they're so career driven. It's a different world."

"You say that like it's a bad thing," Alec replied mildly.

"Is it so wrong to want to see my sons married and settled? I just want you to be happy, darling. It must be lonely going home to that empty flat every night."

"I'm fine, Mother." But her words poked at the empty place inside him. He wondered what his life would be like if he had Ed to go home to every night. If his mother truly wanted him to be happy, surely she'd eventually accept it if Alec ever found the courage to be honest about his sexuality.

They'd reached Alec's family home now, and he was saved from continuing the conversation as he parked in front of the large stone house. They got out of the car as Serena pulled up behind them.

Alec and Caspar carried in their overnight cases, Caspar insisted on carrying Serena's too.

"I can manage it myself, Casp." She closed the boot of the car.

"It's fine. I've got them now."

Their mother directed Alec and Caspar upstairs. "Alec, you're in your old room. Caspar, I put you and Serena in the green room. It's a little larger, so I thought you'd be more comfortable. Serena, let me take you through to the living room."

Caspar looked at Alec and jerked his head towards the staircase. "After you."

Alec led the way upstairs. The rooms they'd been allocated were next to each other at the far end of the landing. As soon as Alec had left his case in his room, he went next door to catch his brother alone.

"What the fuck's going on?" he demanded, closing the door behind him. They wouldn't have long before people got suspicious about their absence, but Alec wanted to know what he was getting into before his brother broke whatever his news was to their parents.

"Okay, well" — Caspar rubbed his hands together nervously — "the good news is that Serena and I are engaged. But the reason we're rushing into it a little is, um, well. It's because she's pregnant."

"Bloody hell." Alec let that news settle in. "Well, congratulations, of course. But are you sure you want to get married? How long have you even known her?"

"We've been seeing each other for a few months. I'm crazy about her, honestly. I already knew she was a keeper even before the baby… that simply made the decision even easier."

"She's so young, though, Casp." Alec reverted instinctively to the nickname of their childhood. "Are you sure it's what she really wants? She doesn't just feel pressured into marriage?"

Caspar snorted. "Serena isn't the type to be pressured into anything. She's nervous about it, of course. This wasn't part of her life plan, but she wants to be with me, she wants this baby, and she's not going to let it stop her following her dreams. She's carrying on with her degree. She might need to study at home for a while, and maybe take a few months off after the baby comes. She's already talked to her tutor, and the university is prepared to be flexible as long as she keeps up with her studies. I can plan my schedule to fit with hers, so one of us will be at home with the baby as much as possible, and we'll hire a nanny to cover when we can't be there. We're going to make it work." Caspar's face showed pure determination.

"And what about you, Caspar. Is this what you want?"

"Yes," he replied simply. He smiled, and Alec could see the excitement and love shining in his eyes. "I didn't know I wanted it till it happened. But I love her, Alec. She's amazing. And I'm excited about being a father. I'm going to be the best dad anyone can be."

"Well, I'm happy for you." Alec stepped forward and gave Caspar a rare hug.

Caspar hugged him back and murmured, "Thanks," into Alec's shoulder.

"God. This means I'm going to be an uncle!" Alec grinned as he pulled away. "You know, although Mum and Dad might be a little disapproving of the shotgun wedding aspect of this, but the fact you're giving them a grandchild will probably cancel out the rest once it sinks in. Mum will be over the moon that one of us is finally breeding."

"I hope so." Caspar chuckled. "I really hope so. Right, come on. I need to go and face the music. They'll be wondering what the hell we're doing up here."

"Good luck." Alec put his hand on Caspar's shoulder and squeezed. "And congratulations again."

"Thank you."

Caspar left the room first, leaving Alec alone for a moment, his thoughts whirling.

It had been years since he and Caspar had connected with this level of honesty and intimacy. Maybe they never had. That awful summer, when Alec had been kicked out of school and was at loggerheads with their father, Caspar had been the one to rub ointment onto the cuts on Alec's back. He'd tried to get Alec to show their mother, in case Alec needed to see a doctor, but Alec had refused. He didn't want his mother to see what his father had done. Caspar had tried to get Alec to talk, but Alec hadn't been ready to discuss what happened with anyone. He'd told Caspar the same as he told everyone else: it was a stupid mistake and it didn't mean anything; he wasn't gay. Eventually Caspar had given up trying to get Alec to open up. Now, Alec found himself hoping he could count on his brother for support when he eventually came out to his parents.

For the first time in his life, he was thinking of it in terms of *when* rather than if. *When did that change?*

Downstairs, their mother had made a tray of tea and was already pouring it into china cups when Alec came in. Caspar was sitting beside Serena on a two-seater sofa, and Alec took one of the armchairs.

Once they all had their tea and they'd finished passing around milk and sugar, Caspar took advantage of a break in the conversation to make his announcement.

"So." He sat up straight and cleared his throat. "Mother, Father, I have some exciting news." Caspar glanced at Alec, who gave him a small smile of encouragement, and then he took Serena's hand and squeezed. Turning to their mother, he said. "I've asked Serena to marry me, and she's accepted." As his parents made sounds of surprise and congratulations, he quickly cut in. "That's not all…. We're having a baby."

Their mother gasped and put a hand to her throat. Shock, a hint of disapproval, and excitement warred with each other on her features for a moment before social convention won out. "Oh my goodness," she managed. "That's wonderful news, if a little unexpected."

"It was a little unexpected for us too," Caspar replied, obviously having decided honesty was the best policy. "I know it's rather sudden. But we couldn't be happier about it."

"Congratulations," Alec's father said. His expression didn't give much away as he addressed Serena. "Welcome to the family."

Serena flushed prettily but met his gaze without wavering. "Thank you."

"When's the baby due?" their mother asked.

"At the end of August," Serena said.

"Do you know if it's a girl or a boy?"

Serena shook her head. "Not yet. We'll find out when I have a scan at twenty weeks."

Alec watched the smile spreading across his mother's face and saw that, as he'd predicted, her excitement at being a grandmother was washing away any of her other concerns. He tuned out of the women's conversation as they branched out into discussing due dates and morning sickness, and he listened to his father and Caspar instead.

"Serena's going to carry on with her degree," Caspar was explaining. "I know it won't be easy on any of us, but we'll manage."

Alec could see the reservation on his father's face, but the older man kept his thoughts to himself for now. Alec was grateful for Serena's sake. He suspected that Caspar would get an earful later.

Sure enough, after they'd finished their tea, their mother whisked Serena off to the small drawing room at the back of the house to show her photos of Caspar as a baby. Once the women were gone, their father pinned Caspar with the full force of his disapproval.

"Good God, boy. She's what… eighteen years old? Couldn't you have been more careful?"

Caspar flushed. "We were careful, Father. But no method of birth control is completely reliable."

Their father shook his head. "If it really *was* an accident."

"What the hell is that supposed to mean?" Casper's face darkened.

"She wouldn't be the first girl to trap a man into marriage, and she won't be the last. You're quite the catch. I assume she knows we're not short of money."

"Her family aren't exactly paupers, Father. She doesn't need my money."

"Hmph. Well, perhaps I spoke too hastily."

That was as close as Caspar would get to an apology. Caspar must have realised that too because he didn't pursue the argument. Instead he said "I thought you'd be happy to be getting a grandchild at last, even if it's a little unexpected."

His father's expression softened a little. "I *am* happy. I'm just worried you're rushing into marriage for the wrong reasons. I don't want to see you get hurt, or for you to hurt that girl."

"I won't." Caspar set his jaw and held their father's gaze.

An understanding passed between them.

The older man nodded, and the tension lifted. "So, I'm going to be a grandfather. It's about time, I suppose." He shot a look at Alec, who tried to keep his expression neutral. "I wasn't sure it would ever happen." He stood, in the slow, careful way of a seventy-year-old man with arthritic knees.

Sometimes Alec forgot how old his father was now. Each time he saw him, he was smaller than Alec remembered. He never matched the formidable image in Alec's head.

"Excuse me. I'm going to the lavatory," his father said. "Then I'm going to find your mother and rescue the lovely Serena from her clutches before she bores her to death with baby photos."

Left alone with Alec, Caspar breathed a long sigh of relief. "Well, that wasn't too bad."

Alec didn't reply immediately. The ticking of the cuckoo clock on the mantelpiece was an insistent beat, reminding him of time passing.

It felt like yesterday that he'd been an eighteen-year-old boy, ashamed and afraid. But he wasn't that boy anymore. It seemed to be the day for revelations, so maybe now was the time for him to finally speak the truth. His heart sped up, racing now, out of step with the *tick-tick-tick* of the clock.

"So, would now be a really good time or a really bad time to drop a bombshell of my own, do you think?" He tried to keep his voice light, but the words came out sharp-edged and a little panicky.

Caspar frowned. "What?"

"I'm gay." Alec threw the words out like stones launched at a window, reckless and risky, and waited to see their effect.

Caspar's expression softened. "I know."

"Wait. What do you mean, you know?" Alec felt slightly hysterical, torn between the urge to laugh or cry, or maybe run away and pretend he'd never started this conversation.

"Well… I never knew for sure, of course. But I guessed."

"When?"

Caspar shrugged and ran a hand through his tousled brown hair. "I never bought your explanation of what happened at school. I mean, I know there were plenty of straight guys who fooled around there, but you never seemed very interested in girls. Apart from Belinda, of course. And I heard on the grapevine that your relationship with her was a lot more casual than you led Mum and Dad to believe."

"And you don't care?"

"Why should I care, Alec? How does your orientation affect me? I always hoped you'd come out eventually because I figured you might be happier if you did. I care about that. I'd like to see you settle down."

Alec snorted; relief and adrenaline flooded through him. "You sound like Mum."

Caspar chuckled. "I do, don't I? I guess I just always felt that you were lonely. Apart from Belinda, you keep yourself to yourself. You're locked up so tight I always felt like nothing could reach you." His face turned serious and he studied Alec, making him flush under his scrutiny. "So why now? Has someone finally got to you? Is there a person behind the sudden desire to come out after all these years?"

Alec sighed. "Yes… no. I don't know. Sort of, I suppose. There's this guy…. But I work with him and it's complicated. He's out, and he didn't want a secret relationship, so it's over almost before it got started. I'm not sure whether it's too late to fix things with him."

Would Ed take him back if he could untangle the lies he'd lived with all these years? Telling his family was only half of it. If he wanted to have a relationship with Ed, he would need to come out at work too. The only way to move forward was one step at a time. Ultimately, Alec wanted to be free of the deception, free of the fear that had kept him prisoner for so long. Even if it was too late for him and Ed, Alec had had enough of hiding. He wanted to come out for himself.

"If he loves you, surely he'll want to give it another go," Caspar said. "If you come out."

"Maybe. I don't know. But I need to do it for me, anyway. I'm tired of living like this."

"So, are you going to tell Mum and Dad today? It seems like the day for life-changing announcements."

Alec drew in a deep breath, filling his lungs as he gathered his courage. "Yes." He stood. "Yes, I am."

"You'll want to be on your own with them for this, I presume? I'll take Serena out for a stroll around the garden while you talk to them."

"Thanks. I don't think I need an audience."

His palms were already sweating at the prospect, but what was the worst thing that could happen? As he and Caspar had joked earlier, being cut out of the will was the only leverage his father really had, and Alec didn't need his money.

Alec knew his fears had nothing to do with money or wills. He'd spent so many years trying to erase the memory of disgust and disapproval on his father's face, and his fear of seeing that again was what had kept him locked in the closet ever since he was a teenager. But he couldn't bear to stay there anymore. Coming out couldn't be any worse than living half a life, denying himself a chance at happiness.

Alec and Caspar found their parents and Serena poring over old photos in the back living room. His father had been drawn into reminiscing too, and they were chuckling over a studio posed photograph of Alec and Caspar aged around six and eight years old. Caspar was smiling beautifully at the camera, but Alec's face was utterly serious.

"The poor photographer tried everything to get you to smile, Alec," his mother said as he came to stand behind the sofa so he could look over her shoulder. "But you wouldn't."

"I remember," he said, managing a tight smile now, unlike his eight-year-old self. "He kept telling me jokes, but they weren't funny. He gave up in the end."

"Serena," Caspar took her arm. "Do you fancy some fresh air? I'd like to show you the gardens."

"Oh, yes. Of course." Serena looked a little surprised to be whisked away so abruptly, but she didn't question it.

Once they had gone, Alec's mother started to tidy up the photo albums.

Alec couldn't bear to wait another second. "Mother, can you leave those for a moment? I need to talk to you both."

Something in his tone made his mother stop immediately. She froze, the pile of albums in her arms.

Alec took them from her and placed them back on the coffee table. "Sit down," he said.

She sat down next to his father, who raised his eyebrows. "Well?" he prompted. "Please don't tell me you've got some girl knocked up too. One surprise grandchild is enough for one day."

Alec laughed nervously. He remained standing. "Um, no. Definitely no more surprise grandchildren." He put his hands in his pockets and clenched his fists, his nails digging into his palms. "I'm gay." The words weren't any easier to say for the second time today.

His mother drew in a sharp breath. His father was utterly silent, his face like stone.

"What do you mean, darling?" His mother finally managed, the words tripping out in a babble of confusion. "What about Belinda? You can't be…." She didn't even seem to be able to say the word. "I don't understand."

Alec felt oddly calm now he was speaking his truth at last. "Belinda and I have only ever been friends." His voice was strong and sure. "I let you believe it was more because it suited me to have you think we were together. But I'm gay. I always have been, and I always will be. I've been hiding it for years, but I'm done with pretending."

The stones were cast and the glass shattered. Alec couldn't take the words back now. He found he didn't want to. He turned his gaze on his father and saw exactly what he'd feared: anger, disgust, disappointment. It was like looking back in time. Only now, Alec wasn't going to deny anything.

His father finally spoke, his voice hard and cold. "How could you? And *why*? Why did you lie to us all these years?"

"Why do you think?"

Alec could almost hear the swish of a belt through the air before it made contact. He recalled the biting pain of the leather hitting his bare skin. But instead of the fear and shame he'd felt then, a surge of anger rose in him. The power of it gave him the strength he needed to hold his father's gaze without flinching.

He's an old man, Alec told himself. *He can't hurt me now. I'm bigger and stronger than he is. I won't let him hurt me again.*

Alec slipped off his jacket and placed it carefully on the back of a chair. Holding his father's gaze, he took off his tie and started to undo the buttons of his shirt.

"What are you doing?" His mother's voice rose, she turned to her husband. "What's he doing, Giles?"

Alec and his father ignored her, their gazes locked, until Alec shrugged out of his shirt and turned around.

"This is why I lied," he said quietly.

His mother gasped, but Alec carried on speaking, his voice gaining strength as the words spilled out of him, fuelled by anger and fierce pride in himself for finally finding the courage to do what he should have done years ago.

"You *beat* me, Father. You treated me as if I was disgusting. You made me ashamed. You made me hate myself for something I couldn't help. It took me years to understand that there's nothing wrong with me. *You* are the one who is wrong. Maybe I can never change your mind, and frankly, I'm not even going to try. This is who I am. Deal with it, or cut me out of your life, because I'm not lying to anyone anymore."

The lines around his father's eyes deepened. He seemed stunned into silence by Alec's tirade. His mouth was a grim line and he stared at the table, not meeting Alec's eyes.

His mother choked out a sob. "Darling, I never knew…. I always believed you when you said it didn't mean anything. Surely you could have told us? We might not have liked it, we might not have understood everything at first… but we would have tried."

"Maybe you would have, Mother. But I'm not sure Father would."

His father was still speechless and his features hadn't softened. Alec couldn't see anything there that looked like acceptance or understanding. Suddenly Alec's anger and courage drained away. He stared at his father, searching desperately for something in his expression that would give him hope. He found nothing. His father wouldn't even look at him.

"Well, that's it, then. I've said my piece."

He was met with silence. His mother gave another muffled sob and pressed her hand over her mouth.

Alec turned and walked away. He closed the door quietly behind him and walked up the stairs to his room. He couldn't stay here tonight. Empty, numb, and utterly drained, Alec picked up his still-packed bag and carried it down to his car. He turned the key and the engine roared into life.

Caspar came running around the side of the house as Alec started to pull away. Caspar blocked his path, shouting at him to stop.

Alec hit the brakes, but he didn't kill the engine. He rolled the window down as Caspar came around to speak to him.

"Alec, are you okay? How did it go?"

"Not great, obviously. I'm sorry to run out on you, Caspar, but I can't stay here. I need to get away. Maybe they need time for it to sink in." Alec was past caring. He just wanted to escape.

"Okay. I'll talk to them. Call me next week." Alec nodded wearily.

"Drive safe, Alec." Casper reached through the window and gave Alec a one-armed hug.

"Bye, Casp."

Alec pulled out of the driveway and drove until he reached a lay-by. He gripped the steering wheel tightly for a moment, trying to breathe slowly and calmly as he weighed up his options. He couldn't bear the thought of going home to his empty flat, and there was only one person in the world who he wanted to see right now.

Before he had time to chicken out, Alec took out his phone and made the call.

CHAPTER TWELVE

Ed was helping cook dinner when his phone rang. His mum was making lasagne, and Ed was in the middle of chopping mushrooms. He wiped his hands on the legs of his jeans before pulling his phone out of his pocket.

When he saw Alec's name on the screen, his heart jumped. He couldn't think why Alec would be calling him unless it was work related, but that seemed unlikely now the deal was finished. "Hello?"

"Hi." Alec's voice was quiet. There was a long pause and what sounded like a sigh.

"Are you all right?" Ed frowned.

"Um… I don't know, really. Sorry, is this a bad time to talk?"

Gemma—chopping peppers at the kitchen table—let out a cackle of laughter at something their mum had said. On his end of the phone, Alec could probably hear the pop music playing on the radio.

"No, it's fine. Gimme a sec, I'll move somewhere quieter." Ed took the phone away from his ear. "I'm just going to take this in my room," he told his mum. "Back in a bit."

She smiled. "No problem. Gem can finish the mushrooms."

Gemma glared at Ed. "Slacker," she called after him as he left.

Up in his room, Ed put the phone back to his ear as he sat on the edge of his bed. His heart was beating fast, and he cursed himself for being like a lovesick teenager over Alec. Just the sound of Alec's voice was enough to send Ed into a tailspin. "What's up?" he asked. "Where are you? I thought you'd be busy with your parents."

"I'm sitting in a lay-by about five miles from their house. I had to leave."

"Why? Alec, what happened?"

"I came out to them, and it went about as well as I'd expected." Alec's laugh was bitter. "My father could hardly even look me in the eye."

"What did he say?"

"Nothing. Well… he asked me why I'd lied, so I told him a few home truths. And then he had nothing more to say to me. He wouldn't even look at me. So I left."

"Are you going back to London?"

"I suppose." There was a long silence, and then Alec's voice was quiet again when he said, "I don't want to be alone."

Ed had never heard him sound so lost. "Come here," he blurted. "I mean… if you want. My mum won't mind." He waited, listening to the soft sound of Alec's breathing. "Okay, no, sorry. Was that a stupid idea? The last thing you want right now is to have to deal with my family. I can come back to London instead if you—"

"No," Alec cut in. "No. I'd like to come to you. You're in Worthing, yes? Can you text me your address and postcode? I think it'll take me a couple of hours to get there from here."

Bloody hell. Ed hadn't expected Alec to take him up on his impulsive offer. But Alec sounded like he could use a friend right now, and Ed wasn't going to leave him in the lurch. "Okay. I'll do that as soon as we end the call. Are you sure you're okay driving. I mean, if you're upset?"

"I'm okay," Alec assured him. "I'm feeling weirdly calm, actually, but the driving will give me some time to think and get my head round things. I'll be fine."

"Right. Well, travel safe, then, and I'll see you later. If you need more directions or get lost, just call me."

"Thanks, Ed. I really appreciate this. Bye for now."

The call ended, and Ed stared at the screen for a moment before pulling himself together and sending the text with the address.

"Shit," he muttered, wondering what on earth he'd let himself in for.

Back in the kitchen, he sidled up to his mum at the cooker where she was stirring the sauce for the lasagne. "So… Mum. I have this friend, Alec, who needs some company. I… uh, I told him he could come here. I wasn't expecting him to agree, but he did. Sorry, I know I should have asked you first, but is it okay if he turns up later?"

Her brow crinkled with concern. "Of course, love. You know any friend of yours is welcome here. I assume he'd rather sleep in your room than on the sofa?"

"Yeah, I should think so." Ed tried to imagine Alec in his childhood bedroom. The image was a strange one.

"Can you make up an extra bed on the floor for him? There's the fold-out mattress in the twins' room that the girls use when they have friends for sleepovers, and a spare duvet and pillows in the top of my wardrobe."

"Okay." Ed turned to go.

"Is he all right, this friend of yours?" his mum asked. "Is there anything I need to know about?"

Ed wasn't sure Alec would be comfortable with him explaining. "I think it's family stuff… a falling-out," he said vaguely. "I don't know all the details yet."

"Okay. You go and make up that bed, and I'll add some more veggies to this sauce to make it stretch a little further."

His mum seemed to pick up on his reluctance to explain more, and Ed was grateful. "Thanks, Mum."

When he got the fold-out bed from the twins' room, he was subject to another inquisition: "Who's coming to stay?" "Do we know him?" "How old is he?" "Is he your boyfriend?"

At least these questions were easy to answer. "He's called Alec. No, you don't know him. He's thirtyish, I think—I'm not actually sure—and no, he's not my boyfriend."

Unfortunately, Ed thought. *But not for want of trying on my part.*

In his own room, Ed fitted the mattress into the space between his single bed and the desk. Once done, there wasn't a lot of floor space left, just enough to move around the extra bed. When he'd made it up ready for Alec, he went back down to help his mum.

Ed's nerves mounted as he waited for Alec to arrive. The thought of him being here was thrilling, yet terrifying too. He looked around at the cluttered kitchen. It was steamed up from the cooking, bright paintings that the twins brought home from school were stuck up on the pin board, and there were dirty fingermarks on the wall and worn patches on the lino floor. It was a far cry from Alec's pristine flat. He wondered what Alec would make of the chaos.

He and his mum were alone in the kitchen now. Gemma had disappeared off with her phone — to text Zac no doubt — and the twins were in the living room with Greg who was watching the football.

"So, how do you know this Alec?" Ed's mum asked. "I've never heard you talk about him before."

"I work with him. He's..." Ed's cheeks heated. "He's actually my boss." He didn't want to give Alec's secrets away, but his mum was bound to ask Alec about himself, so maybe it was better to explain now. "But we're friends too."

His mum raised her eyebrows, and Ed knew the flush on his cheeks was giving him away. "*Just* friends?"

Ed met her enquiring gaze, silently begging her not to press him. "At the moment, yes."

His heart twisted. He wanted so much more than friendship, and he couldn't help wondering whether there was a chance for them now. Alec coming out to his parents was huge. Ed hadn't been expecting that, and he wasn't sure what it might mean.

Her expression softened. "It sounds complicated."

"It is." Ed sighed. "It really is. But I'd rather not talk about it. Alec, he's... well he's not out to anyone. Or he wasn't... so I'm not sure how he'd feel about you knowing."

"Okay, love." His mum nodded in understanding. She put her hand on his arm and squeezed. "I'll be discreet, don't worry."

"Thanks."

Ed's phone chimed with a text. It was from Alec.

Just stopped for petrol. I'll be there by sixish.
Okay, Ed replied.

"He'll be here in about forty-five minutes," he told his mum. "Is there anything else I can do to help with dinner?"

"You can grate some cheese while I make the white sauce and put the lasagne together. Then we need to chop some veg for the salad too."

Glad to have something to keep him busy as his tension mounted, Ed got on with the jobs his mum gave him. He couldn't help his hopes rising along with his nerves, but he felt selfish for thinking about himself. Alec had sounded miserable after his encounter with his parents. Ed was determined to give him some space. If Alec needed him to be a friend rather than a lover, Ed could do that too.

When the doorbell finally rang, Ed nearly tripped over his feet running to answer it. But Alice and Ava beat him to it. Fighting over who got to open the door, they were yelling at each other when they finally pulled it open.

"Hi," Ed greeted Alec over their heads. "Welcome to the zoo."

"Hello." Alec had a carrier bag in one hand and an overnight bag in the other. He was pale and exhausted-looking, and Ed wanted nothing more than to pull him into his arms and hug him hard, but the twins were in the way. "Thanks for letting me come."

"Hello." Alice finally remembered her manners and greeted Alec with a smile. "I'm Alice, and this is Ava."

"Hi, Alice. Hi, Ava," Alec said.

"You need to move, so he can get through the door." Ed gave Alec an apologetic smile. "Sorry."

"What's in that bag?" Alice asked.

"Alice!" Greg's voice came from the doorway to the living room. He shot Alice a warning look. "Sorry about my daughter. Hello, I'm Greg." He stepped forward and offered Alec a hand to shake.

"Alec. Good to meet you, Greg."

"That was rude, Alice." Ava's voice was accusing. "She thinks there might be presents in there," she added conspiratorially to Alec.

Ed stifled a laugh. Alice wasn't known for her impulse control.

"Well, she might be right," Alec said. "But don't get too excited. The petrol station had rather slim pickings when it came to gifts, and the chocolates are meant for your mum rather than you. But maybe she'll share."

"She usually does," Alice said.

"Speaking of Mum, let me take you through to meet her. She's busy with dinner," Ed said. "Leave your bag here for a minute, and we can take it upstairs once we've finished the introductions. Gemma's in her room, but you can meet her later."

He put his hand on Alec's lower back as they entered the kitchen, guiding him through the door.

"Alec, this is my mum, Janine. Mum, this is Alec."

"Hi, Alec. It's good to meet you." Ed's mum came forward and shook the hand that Alec offered.

"Likewise, Janine. I'm so sorry to turn up out of the blue like this. It's very kind of you to let me stay." Alec's cheeks flushed slightly as he spoke, but his voice was soft and sincere.

"It's no problem at all."

Alec got a large box of chocolates out of the bag he was holding and offered them to her. "These are for you. I tried to get flowers too, but the ones at the petrol station were so sorry for themselves I didn't think they'd survive the night." He smiled ruefully.

"These are lovely, thank you." She turned to Ed. "Love, why don't you take Alec up and show him where he's sleeping. Dinner will be ready in about fifteen minutes."

"Sure." Ed was grateful for the excuse to get Alec alone. He could see the tension in his jaw and in the lines around his eyes despite his veneer of charm and smiles. Alec looked as though he was at breaking point.

Ed picked up Alec's bag in the hallway and led him up the stairs. He opened the door to his room and stepped aside to let him go in first. "You're in with me, I'm afraid. We don't have a spare room."

"That's fine." Alec looked around. His gaze lit on Ed's duvet cover and his lips quirked. "Harry Potter?"

Bugger. Ed had forgotten about that. "Blame my mum's sense of humour. She always insists on using this one."

Alec put his bag down on the mattress on the floor. "Is this one mine?"

"No, you have the proper bed, it's probably more comfy. I don't mind taking the one on the floor if you can cope with Harry Potter."

"Harry Potter's fine." Alec moved his bag to the bed and unzipped it. "Is it okay if I get changed? This suit feels a little formal for dinner with your family."

He was wearing something that looked a lot like what he wore to the office. Ed hadn't even registered his outfit, as he was used to seeing Alec like that.

"Of course." Ed went and sat on the edge of the bed while Alec took off his jacket and draped it over the back of Ed's desk chair. Ed watched as Alec dropped his trousers and unbuttoned his shirt. Alec turned his back to Ed as he changed and the parallel lines of the scars on his back were visible in the bright overhead light, a brutal reminder of why Alec was here.

"Do you want to talk about what happened with your parents?" Ed asked softly.

Alec didn't reply as he put on an old pair of jeans and a soft-looking T-shirt. He got a grey jumper out of his bag and pulled that over his head, turning to face Ed as his head emerged. He smoothed his rumpled dark hair back into place before he spoke.

"I'm not sure there's much to say. I told them, so it's out in the open now. But they didn't like it. I wasn't expecting them to." He shrugged, but it was a tense, painful movement rather than a nonchalant one.

"Come here." Ed held out a hand.

Alec hesitated for a moment before moving closer and taking it. Ed tugged him down to sit on the bed, and he put his arm around Alec's shoulders. "It was brave of you to tell them, especially when you knew it would be difficult. How do you feel now you've done it?"

Alec took a shaky breath. "Weird. Untethered… lighter somehow. As if I've been carrying this massive weight around with me, and now it's gone I don't know what to do with myself. But it was horrible. Even though I should have known it would be like that, I couldn't help hoping…." His voice thickened and he leaned in closer to Ed, putting a hand on Ed's thigh as he bit out the words. "I couldn't help hoping they'd be able to accept it. To accept *me*."

His voice broke then, and Ed moved closer, wrapping his arms around Alec as his body shuddered with a sob.

Ed held Alec tight, murmuring words of comfort. "It'll be okay… it'll be okay. I'm sorry." His heart hurt for Alec. He could only imagine how it would feel to face that kind of rejection from the people who were supposed to love you unconditionally. "Maybe they just need some time."

Alec pulled himself together, wiping his eyes roughly as he drew away. He looked furious with himself for his show of emotion. "I'm angry as much as I'm sad," he said. "It's so fucking *stupid*. What difference does it make whether I'm gay or straight? In this day and age, most people don't care. It won't affect my career. It shouldn't be anyone else's business."

"I know," Ed agreed. "Are you going to come out at work too now?" Hope rose, even though now wasn't the right time to ask Alec about what it might mean for their relationship.

"Yes." Alec nodded, his jaw set with determination. He turned to Ed and his eyes were fierce. "No more hiding. No more lies. I'm hoping to be offered a partnership role very soon, and I'm going to tell them before I accept. I want to get everything out in the open at last."

"Wow, Alec, that's amazing. Congratulations." A smile spread across Ed's face. "You kept that quiet. When did you hear?"

"Only on Friday, and it's not official. I hope I'm not jinxing it by mentioning it… but Katherine implied it's very likely."

"Are you sure now's a good time to come out, though?" Ed's stomach lurched. What if Alec's brave decision jeopardised his promotion?

"There will never be a perfect time, but if they're going to make the offer, they can't change their minds and withdraw it because I'm gay. My orientation doesn't affect my ability to do my job. The partners don't need to know the details of my love life or that Belinda was never a real girlfriend. It's not relevant. And I'm done with pretending. I want to be out." Alec took Ed's hands in his, and Ed's heart did a somersault as he stared into Alec's eyes. "I want to be free to have a real relationship… with you, Ed. If you'll have me. Will you give me another chance?"

The raw hope and honesty in Alec's eyes pierced Ed like a knife to the heart and emotion flooded through him. "Of course I will," he managed around the lump in his throat. "God… come here." Ed reached for Alec, curling his fingers around the nape of his neck as he pulled him close.

He pressed his face into Alec's neck and breathed in the scent of his skin. "I'm fucking crazy about you. Saying no to you in Edinburgh was the hardest thing I've ever done."

His words were muffled, but Alec must have heard, because he tightened his arms around Ed as he replied. "I'm fucking crazy about you, too."

Ed turned his head, seeking Alec's lips in a greedy, messy kiss that Alec returned until they finally pulled apart, breathless and grinning at each other like idiots.

Just at that moment, Ed's mum called from downstairs. "Ed, dinner's ready."

Ed groaned in frustration. "God, really? What timing."

Alec chuckled. "I'm starving, though. Come on. We can talk more later." He stood and offered his hand to Ed.

"Talking wasn't all I was thinking about," Ed grumbled as Alec pulled him up.

Alec kissed him lightly on the lips before saying, "Talking is all we'll be doing tonight. We have a lot to talk about, and I'm not fucking you in your mum's house."

Ed's whole body flushed hot at the thought of it, even though he knew Alec was right. He wouldn't be able to get in the mood with the twins in the next room and his mum across the hallway, anyhow. He raised an eyebrow. "There's a B & B over the road. They might have rooms available."

"If everything works out how I'm hoping it will," Alec said, taking Ed's hand again, "we'll have plenty more nights for fucking. Now come on, we're keeping your mum waiting."

Grinning at Alec's words and what they implied, Ed couldn't wipe the smile off his face as they entered the kitchen. It was only when he noticed Gemma's gaze drop to their joined hands and saw her eyebrows shoot up that Ed realised Alec still had hold of his hand.

"Gemma, this is Alec," Ed said. "Alec, my other sister, Gemma."

"Hi, Alec." She dragged her gaze away from their hands and managed a typically awkward teenage smile before looking down at her phone again and hiding behind her hair.

"You said Alec wasn't your boyfriend," Alice's voice piped up accusingly.

Ed blushed and scrambled for words, but his mum saved him.

"Alice, that's enough. You're such a nosey parker. Now, Alec, would you like a glass of wine? I have some red open, but there's white in the fridge, or beer if you prefer?"

"Red would be lovely, thanks," Alec said.

"Come and sit down." She indicated two empty chairs. "And you sit next to him, Ed. Do you want wine too, love?"

"Yes, please."

"Can I do anything to help?" Alec asked.

"No, everything's ready. Just sit yourself down. Greg, can you start serving the lasagne while I pour the wine?"

By the time everyone had food on their plates, Ed had stopped feeling weird about having Alec there. In fact, the strangest thing was how utterly right it felt. Alec was charming — of course — and soon even Gemma was talking animatedly to him about some boy band she was longing to see in concert. Ed caught his mum's eye. She glanced at Alec, and then she smiled at Ed. Ed's cheeks warmed as he read the knowing look in her eye.

Yes. I'm in love with him, he thought, *and it's written all over my face*. For the first time since he'd known Alec, Ed believed this could end well. It was early days, and they had a lot to work out, but the knowledge that Alec wanted a relationship with him was a warm curl of contentment in his chest.

After the meal, and once the clearing up was done, the twins badgered everyone into playing Pictionary. Even Gemma joined in. They drew lots for the teams, and Alec ended up with both twins on the only team of three. Gemma and Greg were together and Ed was with his mum.

"You're not very good at this," Alice said, looking at Alec's attempt to draw a bull. "You need to draw faster, like Gemma."

Gemma had scribbled hers in about three seconds flat, and Greg had guessed it as soon as she added the ring to the nose. Alec had only got as far as drawing something vaguely cow-like.

"Sorry," Alec said. "This is my first time. Maybe I'll get better with practice."

"I expect so," Ava said kindly, taking the pencil out of his hand. "Right, it's my turn to draw next."

Alec did improve a little during the game, but not enough to challenge the experts. Gemma and Greg ended up thrashing the rest of them, but nobody minded because they spent so much time laughing over one another's terrible drawings.

Much later, when the game was over and the girls were in bed, Ed and Alec sat in the living room with Greg and Ed's mum, watching TV and finishing up the wine from earlier. Ed noticed Alec trying to fight back a yawn. The strained look he had worn when he arrived had gone, but he looked exhausted. He'd done a lot of driving on top of an emotionally traumatic day.

"You look knackered," Ed said softly. "Want to head up to bed?"

"Yes." The yawn won, and Alec covered his mouth as he gave in to it. "I'm shattered. Sorry to be so antisocial."

"It's fine," Ed's mum said. "Ed told me about the crazy hours you both work. It's a miracle you can get out of bed at all at weekends. Go and catch up on some sleep."

Ed stood. "Come on."

"Goodnight." Alec smiled at Ed's mum and then at Greg. "And thank you again for making me feel so welcome. It means a lot."

"Anytime," Greg said. "It's no trouble."

Ed's mum agreed.

"Night," Ed said with a wave of his hand.

"Sleep well," his mum called after them as they left the room.

Ed felt weird leading Alec up to bed in his family home. He'd never had a boyfriend stay there before. Well… not since the mates he'd occasionally fooled around with when he was at school, and then his mum and Greg hadn't really known they were boyfriends—or if they did, they'd turned a blind eye. This felt very different.

Ed let Alec use the family bathroom first, and then went to take his turn. When he came back, Alec was down to boxers, a T-shirt, and socks and was just getting into bed.

Ed stripped down too, keeping on his T-shirt and his underwear. "Mind if I join you? It's a bit of a squash, but I thought you could use a hug."

Honestly, Ed could use a hug too. He felt nervous again, uncertain about this tenuous new arrangement between them. He needed the reassurance of Alec's arms around him, the warmth of his body.

Alec smiled and lifted the covers up so that Ed could slide in beside him.

"Is this okay?" Ed asked, fitting himself against Alec's side and putting an arm across his chest.

"It's perfect." Alec's voice was a deep rumble in Ed's ear, and the thud of his heart was comforting and real. The old, well-washed fabric of Ed's Harry Potter duvet cover was soft against the bare skin of Ed's legs, and the warmth from Alec's body was already seeping into his own.

Ed enjoyed it for a moment while plucking up the courage to speak. "I guess we need to talk." He drew back a little so he could see Alec's face.

"I guess we do," Alec replied with a smile.

"So, what you said earlier…." Ed was almost afraid to believe it was true. "You really meant it? You want a relationship—and not a secret one?"

"I mean it. I'm going to come out at work, and I'd like people to know we're an item, if you're happy with that. You're likely to be joining a new department next week, so we won't be working closely together anymore, which is probably for the best. But that means there's no reason we can't be open about our relationship. Workplace relationships are hardly unusual."

"How open are we talking? I mean… are we putting an announcement in the *Times* or what?"

Alec laughed. "There'll be no need for that. I'm going to explain the situation to the partners when I meet them next week. Not because I anticipate it being a problem, but just in the interests of moving forward honestly. Then once that's done, I'll tell the rest of my team. Word will get round quickly after that."

"God." Ed cringed a little at the thought of being the subject of office gossip. "I hope people won't think I'm a star fucker. The lowly minion and the high-flying partner…."

"Don't speak too soon," Alec said. "I haven't got the job yet. But partner or not, they can think what they like. You're a good lawyer, Ed. Your work speaks for itself. And we'll only be a scandal for a week or so. Then something else will happen and we'll be old news." Alec shifted and the hairs on his thighs brushed against Ed's where their legs were tangled together. "So, is it okay with you if I tell people about us?"

The way he said *us* made Ed's insides melt into warm syrup. "Absolutely." He smiled. "It's completely, 100 percent fine."

Alec kissed him, and Ed kissed him back. A sweet, slow brush of lips, filled with unspoken hopes and promises. When they separated, Ed took Alec's hand and held it between them, stroking Alec's palm with his thumb. "What made you decide to come out now? I mean…." He trailed off and looked at their joined hands. "I have to ask. I'm worried you're only doing it for me, that I forced you into it somehow, and if that's true, then I'm sorry. What if I'm not worth it?"

"Ed," Alec said softly. "Ed, look at me." Ed raised his gaze and was stunned by the burning intensity in Alec's gaze. "I'm not going to lie to you. If I hadn't met you, I probably wouldn't be coming out now." Ed flinched. "But—and this is a crucial but—I'm not coming out *for* you. You're a factor, of course, I can't deny it, because I don't want to lose you through my cowardice. By coming out now, I have a chance at the kind of happiness I never imagined for myself before I met you." Alec's eyes were shining and his voice had gone a little hoarse. "I love you, Ed. I'm coming out for me, so I can be with you—for real. Boyfriends… partners… whatever you want to call it. No more risky office sex and stolen moments. I want the whole package."

Ed's eyes prickled. "I love you too," he managed on a choked breath. "God. I can't believe this is actually happening." He kissed Alec again, throwing a leg over him to keep him close in the narrow bed. The duvet slipped and Ed pulled it back up to cover them without breaking the kiss. Then amusement bubbled up inside, fed by the elation of the moment. He pulled away to let it out, laughing breathlessly as Alec frowned in confusion.

"Sorry," Ed gasped. "It just struck me as funny. This is hands down the most romantic experience of my life to date… but the setting leaves a lot to be desired. I can't believe I'm finally confessing my feelings to the man of my dreams under a Harry Potter duvet cover."

Alec snorted and his lips twitched, and then they both cracked up laughing, trying to stifle the sound so they wouldn't disturb the rest of Ed's family, who were probably asleep by now.

When they got their laughter under control, Ed was weak and his stomach hurt from it. They lay in silence then, Ed with his head on Alec's shoulder and his leg still thrown across Alec's thighs.

Alec yawned.

"Are you ready to sleep?" Ed asked.

"Yes. I can hardly keep my eyes open," Alec admitted.

"Want me to go and sleep in the other bed? There's barely room for two in here."

"No."

Ed smiled at the certainty in Alec's voice. "Okay. Well, let me turn the lamp off, and we can rearrange ourselves so nobody ends up with a dead arm."

Once the lights were off, they managed to get comfortable, with Alec spooned up behind Ed and his arm draped over him.

"Mmmm." Ed sighed sleepily. "This reminds me of the first time we slept together. I woke up in the middle of the night, and we were in exactly this position." He wriggled his arse back against Alec.

Alec groaned. "Don't start that. I'm too tired, plus I told you, I'm not fucking you in your parents' house."

"Spoilsport." Ed took Alec's hand and held it tight against his chest.

"Goodnight, Ed," Alec whispered.

"Night."

CHAPTER THIRTEEN

Alec woke to the feeling of a warm body in his arms and the tickle of Ed's hair in his nostrils. He opened his eyes and saw daylight creeping around the edge of the curtains. The events of the day before trooped into his consciousness, and he ran through them until he remembered exactly where he was and why he was here.

He smiled. A sense of freedom and elation swept through him, so powerful that it made him want to shout or sing. But instead he satisfied himself with hugging Ed closer and dropping a kiss onto the back of his head, letting the happiness settle, deep and warm in the marrow of his bones.

As he lay there waiting for Ed to wake, Alec tried to remember the last time he'd felt such a heady combination of joy and excitement. He wasn't sure he ever had—maybe in his final year at school, when he got his offer from Oxford to read law? He'd hoped that he might come out at university and find a way to be himself. But then the shit hit the fan over the incident at school, and fear paralysed him in the fallout, trapped him into choices he'd regretted, yet been unable to escape from.

He breathed in the warm scent of the skin at the nape of Ed's neck. Ed was the key. The key to his lonely closet and the motivation Alec had needed to find the strength to break free of the past, and he would be forever grateful to Ed whatever the future held for them. It was only the start for them, he knew, but Alec was optimistic.

The sound of the television filtered up from the floor below, along with the crashing of crockery and muffled voices. The twins' voices raised in dispute were quickly hushed by Janine.

Ed stirred then and stretched, turning in Alec's arms until they were facing each other. He kissed Alec's lips lightly, then grinned. "Hi."

"Hi yourself," Alec replied, lips stretching in an answering smile.

They stared at each other for a moment, and suddenly Alec *knew*. He knew with a deep certainty that everything was going to work out. This moment would be the one he'd look back on, years from now, and remember as the point in their relationship when the future unfurled before them, bright and full of hope. There would be twists and turns and choices to make, but he knew they'd be travelling that road together.

They spent the day hanging out with Ed's family. Alec was blown away by their easy acceptance of him. Ed didn't try to hide their new relationship, touching Alec often, holding his hand when people could see.

While Alec played on the Wii with the twins in the living room, he overheard the murmur of a conversation in the kitchen between Ed and his mum, but he couldn't hear what they were saying. Ed returned smiling and squeezed in beside Alec on the sofa.

He kissed Alec on the cheek. "Mum likes you," Ed said. "You've passed the boyfriend test. I think it was washing up the breakfast things that did it."

Alec felt inordinately pleased to have the seal of parental approval. "Good to know."

When they left to drive back to London, Greg shook Alec's hand warmly, the twins hugged him, and even Gemma gave him a smile. He said goodbye to Janine last. "Thank you again. It was so kind of you to let me turn up out of the blue."

"It was nothing." Then she added quietly, "I'm sorry things are difficult with your family at the moment. I hope they come around." She stepped forward and hugged him tight. Alec was swamped with a confusing mixture of emotions: warmth, gratitude, sadness.

"Thanks." His voice came out choked and raw. "Me too."

Everyone waved as they drove away. When they turned the corner at the end of the street, Ed settled back in his seat with a sigh.

"Your family are great," Alec said.

"Yeah. I know. I'm lucky."

"I'm afraid I probably won't be introducing you to mine any time soon." Alec couldn't imagine how awkward that first meeting would be. "My brother, yes. But not my parents. Maybe eventually…."

"There's no rush." Ed put a hand on Alec's thigh and patted it. "Give them some space, let it sink in. They might surprise you."

"I guess what I realised this weekend is that even if the worst happens, even if they cut me off and never want to see me again… that's still better than being in the closet. It will hurt like fuck if it comes to that, yes, but it's not like we were ever very close. You can't lose something you never really had in the first place. And at least I still have Caspar."

"Tell me more about him," Ed said. "I'd like to meet him. He's important to you."

"He is. He was great this weekend. Oh! I never told you the other drama." With his preoccupation about his own problems, Alec had forgotten to mention the other surprise revelation to Ed. "Caspar's getting married. That was rather a shock for my parents too because she's much younger than him, and she's pregnant."

"No way!"

"Yes. I'm going to be an uncle."

"Wow. That's exciting"

"I know. Caspar's besotted, and Serena—his fiancée—is great. I liked her a lot. I think it will work out just fine for them."

"Lots of new beginnings in your family at the moment, then?" Ed squeezed Alec's thigh.

Alec reached down and took his hand. He glanced sideways at Ed and flashed him a quick smile. "Yes, it seems that way."

As they drove into the city, Alec was jittery at the thought of their impending separation. He wasn't sure he wanted to let Ed go. He felt fragile and uncertain again, and filled with the irrational fear that once he was alone, Ed might have second thoughts. He knew he was being ridiculous. They could both use an early night to be ready for Monday. It was going to be a big week for both of them, with Ed joining a new team and Alec having a new deal to get to grips with. New relationship or no new relationship, they still had demanding jobs, and that wasn't going to change.

"Do you want me to drop you back at your place?" Alec asked. "You're welcome to come to mine, but—"

"No, I need to be at home tonight, sorry." Ed sounded as disappointed as Alec felt. "I have laundry to do and all my work clothes are there. Plus if I come to yours, I'm pretty sure we'll keep each other awake most of the night."

Alec laughed, even as heat flashed through him at the idea of what that might entail. "Hold that thought," he said, "and keep next weekend free."

"I'm not sure I can wait till next weekend."

Alec wasn't sure he could wait that long either.

Ed gave Alec directions to his flat, and when Alec finally pulled up outside Ed's building, he turned off the ignition and turned to him. "You won't change your mind, will you?" He hated how vulnerable he sounded. But in the spirit of living more honestly, he didn't want to pretend to Ed either.

"No way. You're stuck with me now." Ed's assurance warmed Alec as much as his smile. "Right, well… I should go. I'm going to spend my evening boring my flatmate stupid, banging on about you and how awesome you are."

"I'm going to turn my phone back on and catch up with all the things I have to do next week."

"You turned it off?"

"After the last time I texted you. I needed some time out from the rest of my life."

Ed nodded in understanding. Then he undid his seat belt and leaned across the gearstick to kiss

Alec. Their stubble scratched together, but Ed's lips were soft. Alec didn't want to let go of him, but finally they parted with a mutual sigh of reluctance.

"I guess I'll see you around tomorrow," Ed said. "My stuff is still in your office space, so I'll head there until I find out where they're sending me next."

"I'll see you in the morning, then."

Ed gave him one more lingering kiss before getting out of the car and walking round to get his case from the boot.

Alec waited until Ed had let himself into his flat before driving away.

Alec's answerphone was flashing with three new messages when he got home. "Shit," he muttered, but there was no avoiding it.

He sat on the sofa and listened to them. The first was from Caspar, left last night. "It's Casp. Just checking you got home okay. You're not replying to my texts... call me?"

The second was Caspar again, from just a couple of hours ago. "For fuck's sake, Alec, answer your damn phone. I talked with Mum and Dad. Mum's okay about the gay thing, really. In shock, I think, but she wants to build bridges. Dad... well, it will take him a little longer, but that shouldn't be a surprise. Anyway, Mum's going to call you later."

The last one was from his mother. "Darling, I'm sorry I didn't react better when you told us yesterday, but it was such a surprise. Your father... well. It was even more of a shock for him. You know what he's like. I've told him he's going to have to get used to it, though. And for what it's worth, I think he's ashamed of how he treated you back then. I didn't even know what he'd done. I'm so sorry, Alec." Her voice broke and there was a pause before she carried on. "I know we haven't always been terribly close over the years… but I love you, Alec. And I'm not losing you over this. Una and Philip's youngest boy's gay too, you know? He's engaged to this lovely chap who works in the city. Una was telling me about them over lunch, and she's so excited about the wedding. Philip didn't like it at first, but he came round eventually, and your father will too. Right, I'm sorry, I'm rambling now. Call me… please, and perhaps I can come into town to meet you for lunch again soon?"

Alec listened to the message two more times, and some of the sadness and anger he'd been carrying since yesterday lifted. That was the best reaction he could have hoped for. If his mother was on his side, his father would get there in the end.

Next he turned his mobile back on. As soon as it powered up, it was buzzing with notifications for texts, missed calls, and voicemail.

First things first. Alec texted Caspar.

I'm fine. Sorry I went AWOL. Back home now, speak to you soon.

Then he worked his way through the other messages and emails. Most of them were Caspar; there was a missed call to his mobile from his mum, but she hadn't left him a message. There were also a few work-related emails, including one inviting him to a meeting with the partners on Tuesday afternoon. Alec stared at it, excitement and nerves warring in his stomach. This was the final hurdle. His chance to start afresh and move forward without any more prevarication or deception.

Alec unpacked and showered before he called his parents' number. His palms were sweating as he listened to the ringtone, and when it clicked, he heard his father's voice barking his usual, "This is Giles Rowland. Who's speaking, please?" at the other end.

His heart gave an uncomfortable lurch. "It's Alec. I'm returning Mum's call. Is she there?"

There was a long pause, punctuated by the panicked beat of Alec's heart and the rasp of his father's breath before he finally replied, "Yes, she is."

Alec's heart sank. His father obviously had nothing to say to him.

But then his father spoke again, his voice gruff and awkward, as though the words were dragged out of him. "I owe you an apology."

Blindsided, Alec could only clutch the phone and wait.

"I shouldn't have let you leave yesterday without some resolution. Your revelation was a shock. I think that was obvious." He sighed. "Alec, I wish I could say I'm completely accepting, but that wouldn't be truthful. However, I do understand it's not something you've chosen. It's the way you are, and you can't change it."

Alec felt begrudging respect for his father's honesty, even though his words stung and poked at the anger and resentment Alec had been carrying for years. He supposed this partial acceptance was a start, at least. His father might not be joining him to wave flags in any pride parades soon, but at least they were talking.

"I don't want to change," he said. "I'm happy as I am." And for the first time in as long as he could remember, it was true.

"I'll get used to it," his father said.

"I hope so."

There was the sound of muffled voices at his father's end, and then, "Your mother wants to talk to you," his father told him. "Bye for now."

"Alec." His mother sounded relieved when she came on the line. "Thank you for calling. We were worried earlier when you didn't answer."

"I'm fine, Mother. I was staying with a friend and my phone was off. But I heard your message when I got home. Thank you."

"I've been thinking about it ever since you left, and after what you told us, so many things make sense now. Like why you were so one-track with your work and why you never seemed interested in settling down with a nice girl."

"I think I'll always be focused on my job, but maybe now I'll settle down with a nice boy," Alec suggested, his tone light as he tried to make it into a joke. He gripped the arm of the sofa as he waited for her to react.

"Maybe," she said, her voice soft. "I just want you to be happy, Alec." There was a pause, and then she asked cautiously, "Is there someone? A boy… well, a man?"

"Yes." Alec smiled to himself as he thought of Ed. Saying it out loud made it real again. "Yes, there is."

"I'm glad. I'd like to meet him. The three of us could go out for lunch next time I'm in London, perhaps?"

"Perhaps." It was hard to imagine sitting with Ed and making polite conversation with his mother over lunch, but she was offering an olive branch, and Alec wasn't going to throw it back at her. "Yes. That would be nice. Maybe in a few weeks." He wanted a little more time to get used to his new reality first. "Okay, Mother. I'd better go. I have work emails to catch up on and unpacking to do. I'll call again soon."

"All right. Goodbye, Alec."

"Bye."

He ended the call and tipped his head back to stare at the ceiling. All in all, things were working out much better than he'd expected. He hoped things would go equally smoothly when he came out at work.

On Monday morning, Alec went in early as usual. James was the second person to show up. Looking unusually bright-eyed for a Monday, he greeted Alec with a sheepish smile.

"I'm so sorry about Friday night. I don't actually remember much about the last part, but I made it home in one piece, and I'm guessing you and Ed had something to do with that?"

"Yes. We poured you through your front door and hoped for the best."

"I must have made it as far as the sofa, because I woke up at half six in the morning with CBeebies blasting out of the telly and Charlotte marching a My Little Pony up and down my spine."

Alec laughed. "Ouch."

"Yeah." James grimaced. "Emily wasn't too impressed. But, angel that she is, she let me go back to bed and sleep it off." He sat down in his desk chair and stretched. "So, how was your weekend?"

"It was, um…." God, where to begin? It had been the most intense emotional roller coaster of Alec's life. A simple "good, thanks," would move the conversation on, but James had become a friend as well as a colleague, and it seemed like a good time to start being more honest. "It was a bit of a mixed bag," Alec finally replied, and he didn't try to suppress the smile that spread across his features as he added, "But it turned out pretty well in the end."

"Oh?" James raised his eyebrows. "Sounds interesting. Are you going to leave me hanging with that evasive answer? Or are you planning on filling in some blanks?"

"It's rather a long story," Alec said. "But the short version is that I came out to my parents this weekend." He watched as confusion spread over James's face, followed by dawning comprehension.

"Oh my God, really? So you're…."

"Gay. Yes." Why did so many people find it hard to say the word?

"But what about Belinda?"

"Belinda and I have a rather more platonic relationship than we led people to believe," Alec admitted, ignoring the flush he could feel heating his cheeks. "It seemed easier to let people think we were a couple."

"Wow." James seemed shocked, but there was no disapproval or negativity in his expression, only surprise. "Well, good for you. It can't have been easy telling your folks, I imagine."

"No, it wasn't a barrel of laughs. But my mother surprised me—in a good way—and I think my father will get used to it eventually."

"So, is there a lucky man who was the catalyst for this sudden revelation?" James asked.

Alec cleared his throat, avoiding James's gaze and shuffling some papers around on his desk. "Yes, there is, as a matter of fact."

"Will I get to meet him sometime?"

Alec panicked internally for a moment, warring with himself before opting for a reply that was evasive, but not a lie. "I'd say that's very likely." He changed the subject quickly. "Oh… and James?"

"Yes?"

"I haven't told anyone else at work yet. I'm going to, very soon. But please keep this to yourself for now."

James tapped his nose and smiled. "Your secret's safe with me."

Ed was one of the last to arrive in the office that morning. He hurried in at ten to nine, muttering about delays on the Tube.

Alec heard his voice before he saw him, and the awareness of Ed's presence flooded him with the desire for physical contact. He felt the pull of him, like primal magnetism at a cellular level.

He glanced up, and when he saw Ed's bright smile levelled at him, tried not to grin back too obviously. "Morning, Ed," he said. "Katherine asked me to send you in to see her as soon as you arrived. I guess she'll be assigning you to a new team."

"We'll be sorry to lose you," James said. "Have you got any idea where you're going next?"

"No, but I guess I'm about to find out." Ed paused to take his coat off and hang it on the stand in the corner before going to tap on Katherine's door, which was ajar.

"Ah, Ed. Come in," Alec heard her say before Ed went in and closed the door behind him.

Ed came out about ten minutes later, looking pleased with himself.

"What's the verdict, then?" James asked.

Alec raised his gaze to Ed, waiting for his answer.

"I'm moving over to help with a big case in Employment. It sounds like it should be an interesting one." Ed moved over to his desk and started to gather up a few bits and pieces that belonged to him.

"Need any help?" Jen offered.

She seemed rather crestfallen that Ed was leaving. Everyone in the team had grown fond of him in the few weeks they'd worked together. Alec sympathised. He was going to miss Ed's company during the workday, but he'd probably be able to concentrate better without him.

"No, I'm fine, thanks."

It didn't take Ed long. When he was done, he cleared his throat and said loudly, "Right, well…. I'll see you all around, I guess. Thanks, everyone, for making my start at Baker Wells such a great experience." His gaze flickered to Alec and lingered there.

Alec's heart beat faster, and he schooled his expression into one of careful indifference. "You were an asset to the team, Ed. Thanks for all your hard work. I hope it goes well for you over in Employment."

"If your new team doesn't do Friday drinks, come and join us sometime," Maria said.

"Yes, somebody needs to help Alec get me into a taxi," James said, and everyone chuckled.

"Oh dear, was it that bad on Friday?" Jen asked.

"I fear I made a bit of a tit of myself. I think I had a bad pint."

"A bad pint of cocktail?" Ed teased. "Okay, I'm off. Take care, guys. Good luck with your next deal."

Everyone chorused their goodbyes, and Alec tried not to stare wistfully at Ed's back as he walked away.

CHAPTER FOURTEEN

Monday was a whirlwind for Ed. There was so much new information to take in as he met his new team and was given huge quantities of paperwork to read and digest.

He didn't see Alec again all day and was almost too busy to think about him. But every now and again when he paused in his reading, he'd remember that he and Alec were a couple now, and Ed would almost burst with the excitement of it.

He worked a ridiculously long day, aiming to make a good impression on his new colleagues, so he didn't want to be one of the first to leave. He would still have a good couple of hours reading to get through at home anyway.

When his phone chimed with a text at quarter to nine, Ed smiled when he saw it was Alec. He'd been resisting the urge to text him all day, not wanting to be too pushy. He knew Alec would be as busy as he was.

Are you still in the office? Alec had texted.
Yes.
Have you eaten yet? Alec sent back.

Ed's stomach growled at the thought of food. *No*, he typed and then hit Send.

When his phone rang, Ed answered immediately. "Hi," he said, smiling.

"Hi. So, I'm the last one in my office tonight," Alec's clipped voice came down the line, so achingly familiar that Ed could imagine him at his desk. His dark hair would be rumpled, as it always was at the end of the day, and his eyes would be shadowed with tiredness. "I still have a pile of stuff to read, and I'm craving Chinese food, so I was going to get some delivered here and press on with work rather than carry all the paperwork home. Do you want to join me?"

"For a working dinner? I can bring my reading too."

"It's the best I can offer you tonight," Alec said ruefully.

"I'll take it."

"Is Chinese okay with you?"

"Perfect. I'll be there in ten."

When Ed arrived, Alec stood and walked forward to greet him with a warm smile that Ed felt right down to his toes.

"Hi," Ed said, feeling as shy as if this were a first date. In a way, he supposed it was. Their whole relationship had been kind of backwards, so it seemed oddly suitable.

Alec reached out a tentative hand and cupped Ed's jaw. "Is it okay if I…?"

"Yes," Ed whispered as he closed the gap between them until they were kissing. He lost himself in the slow brush of Alec's lips and the slide of his tongue.

The sound of the phone on Alec's desk made them jump apart guiltily. "That'll be the food. The place on the corner is always really fast." He picked up the phone. "Okay, thanks. I'll come right down." He turned his attention back to Ed. "Sorry." He grinned. "I need to go and collect it from reception."

"Don't apologise for feeding me. I'm all in favour."

They ate sitting at Alec's desk. Ed pulled up an extra chair, and they tucked into spring rolls and chow mein while they carried on reading by mutual agreement.

When all the food was gone, Ed began to yawn.

"Have you got much more to get through?" Alec asked.

"Another hour, maybe. I can always get up early tomorrow instead." Ed yawned again, stretching back in the chair and putting his arms over his head. When he looked back at Alec, he found Alec watching him with unmistakable heat in his eyes.

"Stop it," Ed said, his body already reacting to Alec's expression.

"Stop what?"

"Looking at me with those fuck-me eyes. We said no more risky office sex, but if you keep looking at me like that, I won't be responsible for my actions."

Alec groaned in frustration and adjusted himself.

Ed swallowed, imagining Alec hard in his suit trousers. His mouth watered at the thought. Maybe Ed could just blow him quickly. If they shut the door and were very quiet—

"No. You're right." Alec stood and started to tidy his desk and pack his briefcase. "Another day won't kill us. Let's both go home and get this reading finished. Tomorrow I have my meeting with the partners, so hopefully I'll have something to celebrate. If all goes well, I may end up going for a drink with Katherine after the meeting, but I won't need to stay long. Could you come to my place?" Alec looked as though he was worried Ed was going to refuse.

"Of course." Wild horses couldn't have kept Ed away.

Alec relaxed, and a tentative smile crept over his features. "I can't think of a better way to celebrate... if it all comes off."

"Is there any reason to think it won't?"

Alec shrugged. "Katherine didn't know, but she seemed to think my chances are good. I'm hopeful, very hopeful. But in the spirit of full disclosure, I'm going to tell them about us—if that's still all right with you?" Ed nodded. "There's no way that could jeopardise my position. I know my rights."

Ed chuckled. "I should hope so. Let them try and fire a lawyer for being gay. It would be a bloodbath."

When they'd packed up, they went down in the lift together and walked out into the dark streets. It was a mild evening for late February, with a hint of drizzle in the air.

They faced each other. The streetlights painted Alec's features in sharp relief; the contrast of light and shadow emphasised the jut of his cheekbones and the masculine angle of his jaw. Ed felt weak with longing.

One more day. He could wait one more day.

"I'm going to hail a cab. There's no sense in sharing one, is there?" Alec asked.

"No. I'll get the Tube."

"So, tomorrow...." Alec dug in his pocket and pulled out two keys on a simple loop as he approached Ed. "I've been carrying these around all day, waiting for a chance to give them to you.

This one does the front door, and this one is the inner door to my flat. Let yourself in tomorrow, and I'll get there as soon as I can. I'll text you the address—assuming you can't remember where it is?"

"I'm not that much of a stalker." Ed tried to sound offended but completely failed. His breath caught as he stared at the keys Alec was holding out to him. He put his hand out and Alec placed them in his palm. The metal was warm from being in Alec's pocket. Ed closed his fingers around them. "Thanks."

"Those are for you to keep, by the way." Alec's usual smoothness had deserted him and uncertainty lurked in his eyes. "If you want?"

"Yes. I want."

Alec's expression relaxed a little. "Given the hours we work, we won't see each other much unless we spend time together in the evenings. And I know it's early days, but I hope you'll stay at mine often. It's closer to work, anyway."

Ed grinned. "Excellent. With the promise of a shorter commute, you'll never get rid of me."

Alec moved closer and reached out to straighten Ed's tie. "I have no desire to get rid of you, Mr Piper. Quite the opposite, in fact." He put his hands on the lapels of Ed's coat and tugged him closer. "I want to kiss you goodbye."

"Here?" Ed glanced around. The streets were still busy with people leaving offices late, but they were all walking head down with purpose, or talking on phones. Nobody was paying them any attention.

"Yes." Alec wrapped his arms around Ed and kissed him with a determination and a thoroughness that took Ed's breath away. When Alec drew back, he was smiling. "That'll keep me going till tomorrow. See you in the morning."

He turned, his coat flaring out behind him as he raised his arm and called "*Taxi!*"

A black cab cut across a lane and screeched to a halt. "Sleep well tonight," Alec called back over his shoulder, "because I'm planning on keeping you up late tomorrow."

And then he was inside the taxi, pulling the door shut with a *bang*.

Ed touched his mouth with his fingers, still feeling the ghost of Alec's lips.

Tomorrow couldn't come quickly enough.

Ed's phone rang at six on Tuesday, just as he was finishing for the day. When he saw it was Alec, he picked up immediately.

"How did it go?" he asked, hoping and praying that Alec's news was good.

"I got it!" Alec replied.

Ed could hear the smile in his voice. Alec sounded breathless with excitement. "That's brilliant. Congratulations!"

"Thanks. Even though I was half expecting it, I still can't believe it's really happening. I'm so relieved it's in the bag. I'll be signing the final paperwork on Friday."

"And when you told them—" Ed paused and then lowered his voice. "—about... you know?" He glanced around at his colleagues but nobody was paying attention.

"Not a problem. A couple of raised eyebrows and cleared throats. One of the old goats queried the appropriateness of what he called an 'office fling.' But then Katherine reminded him there are at least two married couples at Baker Wells where both spouses work for the firm. They shut up after that."

"That's brilliant. So, we're celebrating tonight, then?"

"Yes. I'm going for a quick drink with Katherine now, but I'll come straight home afterwards. Will you meet me there?"

"Of course."

"Okay. I've got to go. See you a little later."

"Bye."

Ed felt strangely guilty as he let himself into Alec's building with the keys Alec had given him the day before. He half-expected someone to challenge him, but there was nobody around, apart from a rather self-important grey tabby cat on the doorstep.

The cat tried to push past him as he opened the door, but Ed blocked it with his leg. "Hey, I don't even know if you live here, so I'm not letting you in. Shoo!"

The cat glared and then turned its back on him, holding its tail high with disdain as it stalked off.

Inside, Ed crossed the hallway and let himself into Alec's flat. As he closed the door behind him, memories of the only other time he'd been here slammed into him.

"What a night." Ed smiled to himself, putting a hand out to touch the wall by the front door where he'd blown Alec on their first night together. He remembered how Alec had come all over his face,

225

and he chuckled. That was so fucking hot. His cock was hard just thinking about it. He adjusted himself as he walked down the corridor to Alec's bedroom.

This room was full of memories too. That amazing fuck, the weird intimacy between them in the night... and then the less pleasant memory of Alec ditching him the next morning without so much as a coffee. But things had turned out okay in the end, and Ed was determined they'd be making lots more good memories tonight — and all the other nights that stretched into their future.

Ed stepped out of his shoes and took off his jacket and tie before drawing the curtains. Alec's bedroom was as immaculate as he remembered, so he tucked his shoes away in a corner and draped his tie and jacket carefully over the armchair in the bay window, not wanting to annoy Alec by leaving a trail of mess behind him.

He got out his phone and sent Alec a text, typing one-handedly as he undid his shirt buttons with the other.

I'm here and I'm getting naked. Are you going to be long?

By the time his phone chimed with a reply, Ed was completely undressed.

God. You're killing me. Ed snorted, then watched more words appear. *Just finishing this drink, then I'll leave. Be with you in 30 tops.*

Ed typed back, *Perfect. That gives me time for a shower. I'll try not to start without you.*

Don't you dare.

Showering was pure, perfect torture. Ed was hard before he even touched his dick or his arse. Anticipation and the scent of Alec's shower gel was enough to turn his cock into an iron bar. He resisted the urge to take care of it, knowing it would be all the sweeter if he waited for Alec. He washed thoroughly, biting his lip as he soaped his balls and shaft, and then reached behind to wash his arse. After he'd rinsed the soap away, he carried on touching his hole gently, softening the muscle, imagining Alec's fingers there… or maybe his tongue. His cock jerked, red and straining, and Ed stopped. His whole body had lit up, nipples tight, skin tingling. He needed a moment to calm down before Alec arrived.

Ed turned the water temperature down and breathed slowly, feeling the thud of his pulse in his cock, electric desire thrumming through his veins.

The cold water didn't help much. He still could have hung his towel off his dick after drying himself. He dimmed the lights and got under the covers naked, but the touch of the sheets was too much on his hypersensitive body, so he pushed the covers down and gripped his cock. He held himself tightly, not stroking, but the urge to do so was killing him.

Just then he heard the sound of the flat door opening, and he threw up a prayer of thanks to the universe.

Ed waited in silence and listened to the soft sound of Alec's footsteps coming down the carpeted corridor. He heard him pause by the darkened living room.

"Ed?" Alec called.

"In here." Ed's voice came out husky. He swallowed and took his hand off his cock, putting his arms behind his head and imagining the pretty picture he must make.

"Jesus," Alec said on a hushed breath. "Look at you." He stood frozen in the doorway, his gaze raking over Ed as though he couldn't decide where to look.

Ed felt the journey of Alec's eyes like a touch on his skin, a hot trail of awareness that made his cock flex and leak. "Get over here," he said, his voice tight and needy.

Ed's words spurred Alec into frantic action. He kicked off his shoes and started stripping out of his clothes, tossing them in a crumpled trail as he crossed the room to Ed.

So much for him worrying about the state of his bedroom. Ed smirked, flattered by Alec's obvious desperation to get naked and on top of Ed as soon as possible.

Alec, down to his undone shirt and boxers—and possibly socks, Ed couldn't see from here—reached the bed and crawled over Ed on hands and knees. When Alec crushed their lips together and invaded Ed's mouth with a demanding tongue, Ed stopped caring about the presence or absence of socks.

Alec's hands were everywhere, sliding over Ed's torso, skimming his nipples, and the kiss turned biting and hungry. He moved from Ed's mouth down to his neck, his collarbones, his stomach.

"Please," Ed moaned, lifting his hips and bumping Alec's chin with his erection, looking for his mouth.

Alec buried his face in Ed's groin and licked his balls instead, rasping over the trimmed hairs there with the flat of his tongue until Ed clutched Alec's hair, cursing. He needed more. He needed Alec to move—up to his cock or down to his arse, Ed would be fine with either—but *God*, he needed something. Alec pushed Ed's knees back, spreading him wider, and Ed closed his eyes and cried out at the sensation of Alec's hot tongue licking over his hole.

Alec hummed, and the vibrations nearly sent Ed into orbit. Ed moved one of his hands to his cock and squeezed, trying to stave off the orgasm that was threatening. "Fuck me," he begged. He couldn't wait anymore.

Thankfully Alec seemed on board with that plan. Ed watched as he fetched lube and a condom and got himself ready.

"Do you need my fingers?" Alec asked.

"No." Ed reached for Alec's cock, guiding it to his hole. His body felt strung out, aching with the need for Alec to be inside him.

It had always been like this, even when they were strangers. The physical attraction between them was strong right from the start. But now they were lovers, boyfriends, partners… the combination of the emotional and physical connection was overwhelming.

Their gazes locked as Alec pushed into him. When Alec was all the way inside, he leaned down on his elbows and kissed Ed, slow and sensual as he began to move his hips. They rocked together, kissing, making sounds of breathless pleasure.

"Alec," Ed gasped as Alec kissed his neck, Alec's five-o-clock shadow rasping against his sensitive skin. Ed bucked his hips, groaning as the head of Alec's cock brushed over his prostate, sending sparks up his spine. "Oh God yes. Like that."

Ed lost track of time. He lost all sense of everything apart from their kisses, the drag of Alec's cock inside him, and the building, burning need rolling through him, stealing his words, his breath, and his sanity.

He finally came, throwing his head back and crying out, his body taut and shuddering with the force of his release as he slicked the space between them with his come. He was dimly aware of Alec groaning and stilling, and the pulse of his cock deep inside as he came too.

"Ed," Alec rasped. "*Ed.*"

"Yes." Ed cupped Alec's face, drawing him down into his arms and holding him close.

"I love you so much." Alec's words were muffled against Ed's shoulder.

Ed smiled into Alec's hair. "I love you too." He tightened his arms around Alec. "And I'm so damn proud of you today."

Alec chuckled. He shifted his weight off Ed, only pausing to toss the condom into the bin before lying back down with him. They rolled to their sides, facing each other, and Alec stroked a strand of hair off Ed's forehead. "I'm proud of me too. I can't believe I managed to get here from where I was a couple of months ago. Sometimes I think of that night—our first night together—and I feel like a different person now."

"But you're not. You're the person you always were. You're just not afraid to be that man anymore."

"Yes," Alec agreed, taking Ed's hand and lacing their fingers together.

"How does it feel? Being out and proud?"

"It feels wonderful." Alec smiled. "It's like today is the first day of the rest of my life."

"Or maybe... our lives?" Ed's heart fluttered nervously; was that too much of an assumption?

Alec's grin widened, warming Ed from the inside out. "I hope so."

On Friday afternoon, Alec signed the papers that made it official. He was now a full partner in the firm of Baker Wells LLP. Apart from telling Ed, he'd kept the news to himself until it was signed and sealed.

When he got back to his team after the meeting, Alec was glad to see they were all still there. "Right, chaps. All the drinks are on me tonight," he announced loudly.

That got their attention fast.

"What's the occasion?" Maria asked.

"We're celebrating," Alec said. He watched their curious expressions as they waited for him to elaborate. He smiled, unable to hide his excitement. "Earlier this week I was offered a partnership in the firm, and as of today it's official."

They all burst into spontaneous applause and the room filled with excited exclamations.

"Congratulations!" "Well deserved." "That's brilliant news."

"Well done." James shook Alec's hand and patted him on the shoulder, beaming.

"Thank you, all of you." Alec was touched by their obvious delight at his news. "Let's finish up here as soon as we can, and then you can help me celebrate properly. Champagne all round — unless any of you would prefer cocktails?" He arched an eyebrow at James.

"Never again," James said emphatically, shaking his head.

As the others tied up the loose ends of work and packed their briefcases, Alec texted Ed.

Going for a celebratory drink with the team shortly. Usual place. Join us?

The reply came a few minutes later.

Sure, I'll be there by six.

Alec smiled.

He'd kept his relationship with Ed quiet all week too, even though he'd been bursting to mention it.

Tonight was the night. He was going to tell them, and he wanted Ed there for it. He wanted to prove to Ed that he was proud to be seen with him — show him that Alec was finally proud of himself and who he was.

They'd spent the last three nights together. Ed had gone home briefly after work on Wednesday to get some clothes, which were now taking up space in Alec's wardrobe alongside his own. Alec was planning on suggesting that Ed moved in with him soon. He couldn't see any logical reason to wait.

He had reserved a table at the bar. When they arrived, they took their seats and Alec ordered two bottles of champagne between the five of them — it would be six soon, of course, and Ed would arrive.

Alec waved away the waitress after thanking her, and he opened the bottles himself once she brought them over. "It's half the fun," he said as he ripped off the foil.

"Please tell me you're not going to spray it all over us like a Grand Prix winner," Jen said.

"I wouldn't want to waste it," he assured her.

But when he poured some into the first glass, it frothed over the top and onto the table.

"What was that about wasting it?" Maria teased.

When all their glasses were full, James raised his. "To Alec. Congratulations!"

"Congratulations!" They all raised and clinked glasses, sloshing more of the precious liquid onto the tabletop and laughing before taking a sip.

"Thanks for all your support," Alec said. "You're a great team. I'm lucky to work with you all. I'm not sure I say that often enough."

"No, you don't," James said with a twinkle in his eye. "You should definitely tell us how brilliant we are much more frequently. We never get tired of hearing it."

Suddenly, Alec spotted Ed over James's shoulder; Ed caught sight of him at the same moment, and they smiled at each other. The rest of the world dropped away. James was still talking, but Alec could only watch Ed approach.

"Hi," Ed greeted them.

"Ed!" Maria exclaimed. "This is a nice surprise."

"Here. Luckily there's a spare glass." Jon poured some bubbly for Ed.

"Thanks. I hope you don't mind if I gatecrash?" Ed's gaze flickered to Alec again.

Alec's cheeks were hot and his palms were sweating. Now was the time. "Actually, Ed isn't gatecrashing." His voice sounded like someone else's over the pulse beating in his ears. "I invited him… because I have another announcement to make." He caught James's eye and saw the penny drop. James's mouth fell open in surprise before a huge grin spread across his features. "Ed and I… we're, um—"

"Shagging!" James cried out. "Oh my God, you sly dogs. You're shagging."

Alec's face burst into flames as everyone whipped around to stare at James, then at Ed, and then back at Alec, waiting for him to confirm or deny. Ed was no help at all. He was pissing himself laughing.

"Well, I was going to use the phrase 'seeing each other.'" Alec glared at James.

"I bet you are." James snorted.

"For fuck's sake, James. Will you shut up and let me finish?"

"Sorry."

"We're seeing each other, dating, boyfriends, partners… call it what you like. It's not a secret. Well, not anymore." Alec shot Ed a glance, and Ed's lips quirked.

Alec plucked up the courage to look at the rest of them, scanning their faces for any negative reactions. They mostly looked surprised, but that was fair enough.

"Well, congratulations, guys. I'm happy for you," Maria said, raising her glass again. "I think we need another toast."

"Hear, hear, congratulations," Jen chimed in.

"To Alec and Ed," Maria said.

"To Alec and Ed," the rest of them echoed.

"God, it feels like a wedding," Jon said. "Please tell me there aren't going to be any speeches… but I wouldn't say no to cake."

"No speeches. No cake. And no wedding," Alec said.

"Yet?" Maria raised an eyebrow.

Alec flushed and glanced at Ed, who just grinned.

"To working relationships—of all types." James raised his glass again, still grinning. "I can't believe you kept that quiet for so long. I'd never have guessed."

They raised their glasses and drank again.

"Here, Ed. Have a seat." Jon had spotted a free chair at a neighbouring table and dragged it over, fitting it in beside Alec's.

"Thanks." Ed sat down. "So, what deal are you lot working on now? Is it an interesting one?"

Alec zoned out for a while as the conversation flowed around him. Warm happiness settled in his chest. Life was good. They were crammed in a little with the addition of Ed to the table, and Ed's hand on the arm of his chair was close enough that Alec could easily touch it. The thrilling rush of realisation that he could, and that nobody would be shocked or surprised if he did, was like the fizz of the champagne in their glasses.

Ed was his boyfriend—and everyone knew it.

Slowly, deliberately, Alec took Ed's hand in his own and laced their fingers together, squeezing gently.

Ed turned to Alec, surprise and pleasure on his face. He smiled and squeezed back. "Hey," he said quietly. "You okay?"

"Never better," Alec replied.

And it was the truth.

About the Author

Jay lives just outside Bristol in the West of England, with her husband, two children, and two cats. Jay comes from a family of writers, but she always used to believe that the gene for fiction writing had passed her by. She spent years only ever writing emails, articles, or website content.

One day, she decided to try and write a short story—just to see if she could—and found it rather addictive. She hasn't stopped writing since.

Connect with Jay
www.jaynorthcote.com
Twitter: @Jay_Northcote
Facebook: Jay Northcote Fiction

More from Jay Northcote

Novels and Novellas
Cold Feet
Nothing Serious
Nothing Special
Nothing Ventured
Not Just Friends
Passing Through
The Little Things
The Dating Game – Owen & Nathan #1
The Marrying Kind – Owen & Nathan #2
Helping Hand – Housemates #1
Like a Lover – Housemates #2
What Happens at Christmas

Short Stories
Top Me Maybe?
All Man

Free Reads
Coming Home
First Class Package

Audiobooks
Cold Feet
Nothing Serious
Nothing Special
Nothing Ventured
Not Just Friends
Passing Through
The Little Things
The Dating Game – Owen & Nathan #1
The Marrying Kind – Owen & Nathan #2

Printed in Great Britain
by Amazon